Profane Feasts

Profane Feasts:

American Edition

story-chapters by
Tom Tolnay

atmosphere press

Published by Atmosphere Press

Cover illustration taken from Münchener Bilderbogen, München, 1890

ISBN 979-8-89132-043-7

Atmospherepress.com

Contents

Prolog

With increasing numbers of Greeks wandering around metropolitan New York, the author noticed many of them seemed to be employed as corporals of the service industry—park attendants, dog catchers, supermarket clerks and, especially, dishwashers, waitresses, and short-order cooks. This circumstance led him to wonder: How did it come to pass that these custodians, busboys, and counter girls are the last vestiges of ancient Greece's architects of Western Civilization?

To explore this question informally, he began writing story-chapters which followed the exploits of one Greek family transplanted to Brooklyn, NY as it wrestled to make sense of life in America from the 1960s to the end of the 20th century. He used family feasts at Christmas, Easter, Thanksgiving, a wedding, and a funeral as milestones in their journey, and identified these feasts as profane because of the unholy manner in which they were conducted. The "profane feasts" herein are narrated by Alexandros Dropolous, Jr. as he passes from childhood to young manhood and, ultimately, to his own wedding feast and the baptism of his son.

Whether their journey had been carefully planned or pursued intuitively, the author believed these Greeks in America were, in effect, using their classical history as a kind of modern-day Trojan Horse. Their idea was not to topple our government which, after all, is held together by Greco-Roman ideas, but to replace their own, long lost greatness with the American dream by inserting themselves, patiently and unobtrusively, into one household, one coffee shop, one school, one house of worship at a time. Alex's Hestiakos/Dropolous clan was unwittingly part of this scheme.

Of course the Greeks were vastly outnumbered in this epic struggle by the broad assortment of nationalities which constitute American society. By the 21st century, though many trampled traditions had been left on the social battlefields, it became obvious that born-and-raised, second-and-third generation Americans would prevail. But it was also apparent, because this imaginary Greek family and their real-life counterparts had fought so tenaciously to uphold their respective heritages, that millions of Americans would be including more grape leaves, black olives, and goat cheese in their diets than ever before.

Aunt Harriet's Odyssey

Not counting Odysseus, Alexander the Great, and my Aunt Harriet, Greeks have little heart for wandering. Rather than tear their bodies away from land that is the fiber of their being—a paltry allotment of stony soil, they gave it poetic names, such as the Peloponnesian Peninsula, whitewashed their houses to reflect more light out of the sun, learned to pick the bones of fish clean, and entertained themselves by dramatizing their conditions in marble, drama, and song. With this arrangement they remained more or less content until the twentieth century. Squeezed between vanishing natural resources and widening political turmoil, the Hellenics found their parcel of terra firma growing stonier and more constricted all the time, and were forced to accept, at long last, that their greatness as a people had wafted away like golden sand into the aquamarine waters of the Mediterranean. It must've been then, around mid-century, that they hit upon the scheme—subconsciously, at very least—of superimposing what was left of their classic ideals on the brash, nouveau culture that had arisen in the west. Better to latch onto an already thriving society, they seemed to be thinking, than to wait another two thousand years for the pendulum of sovereignty to swing back to Greece. Multitudes of Greeks set sail not to Persia to battle the descendants of Darius at sea, but to America for a more subtle tug-of-war at the hot dog carts, hamburger stands, and coffee shops of New York City. My grandmother, carrying her daughter Delphinia, the fetus of what was to become Harriet and, many months later, my grandfather, were in attendance.

Once she had set foot on the eastern edge of the North American continent, my grandmapou, respectfully known as Ya-Ya, embraced her own heritage doggedly, feeling no need whatsoever to roam where the buffalo used to roam. Besides, the city had five boroughs to choose from. Toward Staten Island she looked with distaste: It was across the wide, murky mouth of New York Bay, and she'd had enough sea slapping in her ears to last a generation. Manhattan was too vertical, not to mention too crowded with immigrants from other cultures, for her flat consciousness and homogeneous perspective to flourish. The Bronx to the north seemed as far off as The Klondike. And Queens, at first, sounded too high and mighty for her humble family. But in Brooklyn she found a ground-floor parlor and bedroom—cheap, where one could step out onto a fifteen-foot square patch of stony, barren earth without being noticed. Just like home! Ya-Ya purchased a packet of morning glory seeds, and in the borrowed shade of branches that reached over from the next, fenced-off yard, as little Delphinia tried and tried to mold mud pies out of that feeble stuff, my grandmother awaited the wonder of bringing new life into the New World. At the time she was also waiting for her husband to join her in America, thereby acknowledging not merely the audacity but the sagacity of her relocation.

The miracle of birth occurred on schedule, but something got reversed in translation. Young Harriet never took to learning Greek, or cultivating marigolds, or heeding her parents. As soon as she was a ripe young creature she ran away from home, embarking on a more or less continuous odyssey back and forth across this broad and, as she learned, diverse country, becoming in the process much too American to contribute to the Greek conspiracy. Some say she had itchy feet all her life because of that transatlantic trip she took, awash in her mother's womb. But Aunt Harriet has always maintained she traveled in the name of love. With six husbands to her credit or, as most think, discredit, there always seemed to be one man or another to run after—or away from. Too bad she wasn't satisfied with hopping to Detroit or Chicago, where clusters of the next generation of Greek-Americans had dug in. Postcards arrived from black heads on the map the family never knew existed, and which no Greek had ever journeyed to before, so far as we knew. Still we got to see quite a bit of her. Whenever her latest mate died off, or grew dull, or neglectful, Harriet would appear on Ya-Ya's doorstep in Flatbush, clutching a child by the hand, a couple more wavering bow-legged on the porch, an infant tucked between her breasts, and possibly one in her pouch.

* * *

Ya-Ya and grandpapou had been lucky enough, or "visionary" enough, to latch onto a sagging, triple-decked, former old ladies' home early in their American occupation. Whenever anyone else had gazed upon the heap—complete with front-loaded, rusted fire escapes, they visualized a wrecking crew swinging sledge hammers in a cloud of dust. When grandpapou had gazed upon it, he visualized his wife and he strolling through a fancy palace on the Ionian Sea, while young maidens with blossoms in their hair were making their beds and sweeping the floors. With a few hundred dollars down payment, and a decade of carpentry, plumbership, electricianship, plastermanship, roofmanship, and other general patchmanships, the place stood more or less on its own legs—not a palace, certainly, but serving a single family again as was intended by its original builder: upright if not sturdy, dry if not warm, cheerful if not handsome, and shorn of excess walls and outriggings. What lent the slanted structure its cheer was not the yellow paint smeared over its outer shell but the children who were periodically dropped off there by Harriet since it was the only family holding large enough to contain them all . . . until such time as she had leashed a new father for her diverse litters, or had cooled down enough to go back to the previous one for awhile. In the meantime *my* father's ears would remain bright red until she disappeared again. But he couldn't do much about her: Harriet had wasted much of her childhood in that house and therefore had history on her side. Worse yet, since the place had been recovered from the junk heap by grandpapou and Ya-Ya, the Hestiakos family looked upon my father more as its caretaker than its resident.

I can understand why the family might have felt that way. I can understand why my father might have felt enraged. What I have never been able to grasp is how Aunt Harriet managed to convince half a dozen breathing, presumably sane men to enter the bonds of holy hammerlock with her. The mystery deepens with one steady, hard look at her; one brief conversation. That is not to say she has a wart on her nose or speaks with a lisp. Harriet is simply more distinctive for the physical and mental graces she does not possess than for those she does: My aunt does not brandish shoulder-length, silky blond hair—more it's the color and texture of a gray squirrel's tail; she does not understand why left-handed pitchers have a better out-percentage against left-handed batters; she does not have sparkling emerald eyes—they're closer to the hue of dried mud; she does not step across a room with the drift of a ballerina; she does not have a flair for telling a spicy joke; she does not have swelled, uplifted breasts; she does not—let's be honest—have any of the qualities you'd expect of someone with her romantic history. Aunt Harriet the woman could be summed up in two words: "So what!" Be that as it may, she has always proved to be extraordinarily enticing to men. Even as a girl, they say, boys would come "buzzing 'round," leaving penny candies and little notes on her desk; following her home after school, chucking pebbles against her bedroom window, scratching her name in the wall above the boys' urinals.

Each time she burst in on us on Columbus Day, Valentine's Day, Washington's Birthday, or in the middle of any old morning, noon, or night—setting off a rumble of mutterings from my father, it reawakened in my mind this question: How in the name of Zeus does she do it? Though her eyes had sunk a little further into her skull upon each return, and her voice had turned a note or two more acidic, I knew, we all knew that sooner or later Aunt Harriet would find another victim hiding under a barstool, or buying socks in Gimbels, or walking a dog in the park. Somewhere, somehow she'd fetch him, usually marry him, and haul him off to some God-forgotten train station that was surrounded by factories or cornfields.

If anyone in the family understood her powers better than I did, they never discussed it within earshot of me. An occasional flash of teeth or bend in their voices eventually led me to consider her mystique may have been based on technique—that this plain-Jane body and soul, who looked more like a maiden aunt than a woman with enough husbands to qualify as a Hollywood movie queen, was one of the most skillful lovers to pound the sheets since Helen of Troy took on the Grecian navy. Since that possibility struck me as remote as the village in which my grandparents were born, my mind floated into more ethereal realms for an answer to this enigma: I imagined my aunt released a kind of spiritual essence into the atmosphere which somehow worked its way into the hearts, minds, and bodies of disengaged or, for that matter, engaged men as well; and before they knew what had come over them, they found themselves lugging home two gallons of milk, three dozen eggs, two pounds of butter, three loaves of bread.

* * *

I wasn't on earth at the time so I never set eyes on hubby number one, Benny the Nipper. As the story goes, despite being a drunken bum he was a good provider, at least in the beginning. Benny could get beef and mutton wholesale through the butcher he worked for in Seward, Nebraska. And if he happened to spend all his paycheck on whiskey, which often was the case, he simply tucked a few chops into his pockets: Harriet and the babies ate like Minoan royalty. Then Benny got caught with a couple of frozen steaks in his pants and was chased into the streets—one step ahead of a meat cleaver. Jobless, Benny began to spend the extra time on his hands with a few pals, all of whom happened to be bartenders. Two months later he turned up in snow-skinned Memorial Park, coughing, hugging a tree—hopefully for warmth rather than affection: It was pneumonia. Harriet hung around for the tears and the flowers. Having married against her parents' wishes, she couldn't go back home . . . not until she had a sad story to tell them. Now she had one. The bottom line of that impulse was two and a third kids, half a year behind in rent, and a pair of dried-out, pilfered chicken thighs in the icebox.

Husband number two was dubbed Timothy the Meek by the family. He was part Austrian, part Siberian, and, according to Harriet, part fish. They tell me Timothy was the gentle one, the considerate one, the easy-going one—and the first one to be dropped by Harriet like a cold cod. Seems it drove my aunt pragmatic to see her limp and lanky husband swimming about utterly unflustered by the turbulence of six goldfish, four kids, three cats, two canaries, and one dog, all stirred up in a four-room fish tank outside Manassas, Virginia. Number two worked at one of those gray steel desks behind one of those blurred glass partitions at one of those government agencies with a name too long to remember. Had Timothy not been cursed with such a temperate personality, and such a puny salary, he might have hung on to her. But four years after an efficient courtship—twelve days in his mother's mobile home in Biloxi, Mississippi—and brisk ceremony in Bowie, Maryland,

Harriet realized it was never going to get any better. After feeding his goldfish to the cats, and setting the furry beings free, she carefully folded her prettiest print dress, stuck clean socks for the kids in her pocketbook and, toting a cage of canaries, followed a deep-tonsiled, mustachioed underwear salesman halfway across the country.

Parland the Peddler had many fine impulses beyond the amorous, the least prominent of which must've been the desire to be bound by law to a female with four brats, two canaries, and a mutt. Nevertheless, at a motel somewhere along the Texas panhandle, Harriet had roped the snappy-talking rascal in checkered trousers, and had him standing before a sleepy-lidded Justice of the Peace, stunned but singing "I do!" And the connection lasted longer than most expected. As they say, however, you can lead a traveling salesman to a little white house with canaries, but you can't keep him caged in, refereeing a pack of kids who spent most days bouncing off the walls with vocal chords at full throttle. Ironically it was number three's tendency to hit the road that led to his tragic, utterly conclusive crash. While the steel girders were not even budged on the trailer bed of the truck, the sample case of long johns in his station wagon was strewn halfway to New Orleans, his destination. Why Parland was trying to sell long johns in Louisiana is another of the mysteries he left behind. Whether this was his way of escaping a fate worse than oblivion, as a neighbor, Mrs. Cyclethes, slyly suggested to my mother, we have no way of knowing. All that's certain is that a few days after the closed casket burial Harriet and company showed up at Ya-Ya's place in Brooklyn, just in time for dinner.

* * *

Albert the Bleak, who ran a one-room insurance brokerage, apparently wooed Harriet by showing up for their first date with a money-back life insurance policy made out to her. His skin was pale as white bread, and he had what looked like cigarette tobacco for eyebrows. By this time even the more charitable members of the family were speaking with a pinch of cynicism about Harriet's marital practices. Aunt Delphinia and my father led the pack. "Harriet the Nomad," she called her. "Harriet the Brazen," he called her. That kind of talk, I suppose, was to be expected. What really riled up my mother was Aunt Merrula's references to the evil Harriet had brought upon everyone she'd married. When my mother declared that was a wicked thing to say about her own sister, my aunt whipped out a picture postcard of a Lutheran Church beneath too-blue a sky in Fergus Falls, Minnesota. In handwriting as frail as strands in a spider's web, Aunt Harriet informed her sister and, thereby, the entire family, that Albert had gone into a coma due to "a trouble of the heart." No one in the family has been able to clear up that ambiguity: whether Albert had sustained a heart attack or had shut down because of some affair of the heart on the part of Harriet. Either way, Uncle Albert handed over the baton shortly thereafter. But at least he'd left Harriet with a tidy insurance payoff that would keep her and the kids in burgers and beans while she hunted down a replacement. Two weeks later there she was, the yellow cab rattling at the curb, a worried glaze over the driver's eyes as he counted the kids marching up the steps to our place in Flat-bush.

Partner number five was imported from Athens; not the one in Greece, the one in Ohio. Nevertheless he presented himself as a full-blooded Hellenic. Plus his name, Christos, automatically made us think of him in a holier light. Harriet had "bumped into" him at a bus terminal in St. Louis some years before, she explained. The encounter must have made a deep impression on her: A day or two after her arrival in Brooklyn from Minnesota she scratched out a postcard of the Fulton Fish Market inquiring as to whether he was still interested in marrying her. A few weeks later there he stood on our door-step, hairy, nervous, eager, dark as overdone toast, and lumpy as a sack of figs. "I woulda been here sooner," he apologized with a wince, "but I had business to take care of." Apparently it had taken longer than he'd expected to sell his paneled truck, his restaurant, his house. Christos entered our home and our lives clutching two pasteboard suitcases and spouting plans to launch still another successful eatery "out east." My mother Evangelina felt encouraged—he was Greek, he was ambitious, he was earnest, he had cash, and he didn't seem to be drunk. My father felt enraged.

To his credit Christos the Loyal did exactly as promised; within six months he staged a gala opening of the Acropolis Cafeteria on Metropolitan Avenue, and shortly thereafter hauled Harriet out of my father's favorite armchair over to St. Demetrius, located in Queens but within shooting distance of Brooklyn. But Harriet never showed up for the wedding. Christos had already paid in cash—or so my mother claimed—for a two-family house near Victory Park in Queens. The squat, wooden frame abode had ample space for their mob, a brick stoop and, as Christos announced proudly, "a farm to grow grapes." Actually it was only a plot of crumbly dirt out back, and Harriet had never liked the soil: "It ruins my fingernails." After less than a year he lost the house, and my aunt found she didn't care for Christos nearly as much as she had on that rainy, lonely, adventurous night in Missouri years earlier. There she was on our porch again, surrounded by her off-spring: enough by then to start a small orphanage. This time, however, her almost hubby was right behind her.

"My darling come back!" Christos pleaded, his eyes red and wet. "What did I do? What did I say?"

"Nothing," said Harriet icily. "You did nothing. You said nothing." And she slammed the door shut on him.

Though my mother was not one to butt in on other people's affairs, she was curious, not to mention concerned: "Why, Harriet?"

"He has hair growing out of his ears."

"For that you leave Christos alone?"

"He gets under my feet."

This was a reason my mother could understand, but she still didn't think it was enough. "Maybe you could watch where you walk?"

"He expects me to settle down in that broken down house in Queens the rest of my life!"

Harriet moved into our house, and the blood shot up my father's neck like mercury in a thermometer struck by direct sunlight. The weekend after her return to Flatbush she started going out into Manhattan at night, while the kids raced through the house and my parents raced after them. On several occasions over the next months Christos the Loyal waited out on our porch for Harriet to return, and on two of those evenings he felt obliged to raise his fists to the suitor who accompanied her. But they were small, loose fists, and neither of the elderly gentlemen could find it in their souls to take him seriously. Nor could Harriet. She continued to rummage the city for candidates. Though she'd dyed the gray out of her hair, and taken to applying the lipstick thickly, it was becoming more difficult for her to make steady connections, and a year passed before she dragged home the character who would turn out to be daddy number five. Uncle Augie was a balding, pasta-packed, nattily gotten-out crook. Well, I shouldn't come right out with my suspicions. Put it this way, he wore white ties over black shirts, lit Cuban stogies with a gold gas lighter, flashed diamond-studded rings on both hands, and was never known to do a lick of work, honest or otherwise. But he loved children, and had been "too busy" doing who-knows-what to have any of his own.

After uttering the necessary words before the appropriate witnesses, Augie the Crook moved kids and kaboodle off to the outskirts of Miami Beach "to be close to my business interests." Over the next few years we didn't get to see much of them. But we saw plenty of Uncle Christos. Though he and Harriet had lived apart for years, he kept bringing his sad, circular eyes to the big old house in Flatbush; he is, after all, still Greek and technically still part of the family's history. In some ways, mostly for his loyalty, I suppose, he is admired more than our own Harriet. But the main reason we invite him to dinner, and ask his advice, and buy him a spotted tie each Christmas, is because we feel partly responsible for the poor condition of his life. This is why Ya-Ya invited Christos to come live with us.

* * *

The summer after we had buried my father safely out of Harriet's way—in Cyprus Hills Cemetery, within earshot of the roar of the Jamaica BMT subway, my aunt, sweating and solemn, the brim of her purple hat banged up, appeared in Brooklyn with what remained of her brood—two or three of them—now taller than my aunt, had taken off on her. Wavering in the yellowed light of that swaying, faint bulb on the porch, her hair soggy with travel, she said: "Evangelina, I left Augie."

Bulky and flat-footed at the doorway, my mother looked past her sister out onto the street, staring into our old Plymouth by the curb, as if she saw her husband seated at the wheel again, waiting for her to wobble down the stairs so they could pick up Delphinia and drive off to an evening of Bingo at St. Demetrius. At last she spoke: "You can't come in."

My cousins must've been too numb to understand that statement could mean an extension of the horrors of running away they had just undergone. Personally, watching from the living room archway, considering the years my mother had argued with my father on Harriet's behalf, I was shocked:

For one thing, my father was no longer around to complain about Harriet so it would've been easy to let her in. As for my aunt, she seemed unable to conjure up that solemn stare of hopelessness which had worked on my mother so many times before. But then she must've reached deep inside her soul for a scrap of spirit, like a boxer struggling up off the canvas at the count of nine. "I am your sister," Harriet said, "and we are tired." My aunt took one step forward.

"I know what you are," said my mother with the breathlessness that comes from going against family bonds. But she did not budge out of the doorway.

"Evangelina, these are your nieces and nephews," Harriet stated. "What have they ever done to you?"

"Nothing they have done to me," she replied, her voice shaking. "You can not come in."

"This is my house, too!"

"Not for long time," said Evangelina. "And never again."

Aunt Harriet's fading brows arched toward the center of her longish face. Her narrow shoulders seemed to grow narrower. Her pointy nose pointier. "Where can we go if you turn us away?"

"You must go where you belong. Back to your husband."

"He's a brute! I won't live with him another minute."

"For once in your life, Mrs. Correggio, you have to find a way to live in peace with your husband."

"I'd rather live with dogs!"

"Harriet," said Evangelina, "you'd better take a look in the mirror."

"What's that supposed to mean?"

"Always you cannot run, run, run," said Evangelina. "One day you'll have to stand still so we can carry you away and bury you."

The kids began to stir, finally realizing their mother might've led them down a wrong turn in the road.

"What kind of thing is that to say to me?" crowed Harriet, her voice shredding. "What kind of sister are you?"

The double-barrel blast shook my mother, but she did not back up, holding firm in honor, I suppose, of her dead husband.

"Come, children, I must have the wrong house," said Harriet without moving, looking past my mother into the dim hallway at me. One part of me wanted to cry out, *Let them in!* but a deeper instinct gave in to my mother's, and my father's, wishes.

At last Evangelina responded: "You are right; this is the wrong house for you."

Maybe my mother had been out of the room the day my aunt made a statement that has stuck in my mind for years: "An unhappy marriage makes the devil laugh." Otherwise Evangelina might've gone along with her sister just one last time. Living in marital misery, it seems, was against Aunt Harriet's religion.

* * *

Less than a week later we heard that Harriet had visited Christos the same evening, before he'd moved in with us. Her brood had moved in with him, sleeping on the floor of his apartment. Except, quite possibly, for Harriet, who may have found her way to his mattress. The next morning my aunt borrowed "a few dollars" from him, and he drove them all the way to Manhattan. At Penn station he bought them hot dogs and Cokes, kissed the kids on the forehead and, no doubt, cried all the way back to Queens. Through the long day their train had clack-clack-clacked in and out of Maryland, Virginia, the Carolinas, and eventually squealed to a stop in the Sunshine State. Another cab she couldn't afford carried them safely, if blinded from fatigue, home.

Augie, equally weary, and with hot tears, hugged them all

at the same time and swore to speak kindly to his wife till death did them part—swore to do anything she asked. And he apparently made good on his promise. Though he must've hated to distance himself from his operations in the lotion and liquor capital of America, a few months later Augie called up the Seven Santini Brothers and had them load a split-level full of stuff into a moving van. The Greco-Roman plaster lamps and the pseudo-marble birdbath were hauled north so his bride could feel she hadn't entirely abandoned her own kind. Specifically they moved to Greenpoint, which is not an especially green point, but which had the strategic advantage of straddling Queens and Brooklyn; that way she could be close to her sisters and, charitably, not far from Christos either.

Augie and Harriet have been together ever since, and the wisdom, the courage my mother displayed that evening surfaces in my thoughts from time to time. There are those who claim Harriet has never been happier since she became more like one of us, keeping her feet planted on firm earth for a change and watching life go by, instead of trying to pass by life as in a race against the years. For we all know who wins that race, in the end.

A Gaggle of Greek Braggarts Living with Poverty

My family is a "gaggle of Greek braggarts." I call them "braggarts" because, whenever handed the slimmest opening, they would drop the name of an ancient hero or three into their prattle with a neighbor, mail lady, shoe repairer, garbage truck driver, or any other innocent bystander: *Aristotle, Diogenes, Epicurus, Heraclitus, Plato, Socrates,* and so forth. It's not that my mother (Evangelina), Uncle Stavros, Cousin Peter, my pretend-uncle Christos or, for that matter, me—Alexandros Dropoulos Jr.—ever actually sat down and read a few pages of the brooding wisdom left behind by these wise guys. At most we may have read *about* them in school or heard them mentioned in the playing out of a Greek legend in a *movie.* Even so, the names of these illustrious thinkers would skip off their tongues freely and frequently. "Plato was a cool cat!" "Socrates dreamed big." "Aristotle taught us that money is the measure of all things." But I can't really blame my family for expressing themselves in this manner. After what had become of Greece's golden age of enlightenment, these modern day Hellenics didn't have much to brighten their immediate prospects, so they boasted about their 2,000-plus year old, magnificent past. As it turned out, this remote connection to their Olympian history was the only wealth my family ever possessed.

Though rich in their imaginings, these braggarts were "dirt poor" in their pockets. I call them "dirt poor" because, for one thing, we had only a shovelful of earth sprinkled over the diddly-squat plot out back of the warped boards, crinkled siding, and shaggy shingles which kept our abode from crumbling back into the earth. Six of my mostly pure-bred clan squeezed themselves into the five-room apartment downstairs, while the Egyptian mother, Irish father, and two mixed-breed squirts ate, slept, and prayed between slabs of punctured wall boards on the upstairs floor. But I can say, in all honestly, that our empty-handed condition never got in our way all that much mainly because not one of us ever looked the harsh reality of our poverty straight in the eye.

The occupants of five or six houses of comparably broken-down construction on our block were able to claim dominion over slightly bigger plots of stone-clotted soil upon which to nurture a stalk of tomato or patch of cucumber. On our particular patch of that crumpled crust my grandmapou, affectionately known as Ya-Ya, would thumb a row of carrot and string bean seeds into the gritty layer with Mediterranean ardor, while up against the house she'd scatter a palmful of marigold seeds as if to remind her family that beauty mattered even when you were teetering on the bottom rung of the financial step ladder.

This stark neighborhood was a new living arrangement for us, having been forced to clear out our closets in the Flatbush section of Brooklyn. Shortly thereafter, providentially, my mother managed to stumble upon a couple of empty closets at a much lower rent in Jamaica, Queens. In this neck of New York City, we were mostly surrounded by slabs of concrete underfoot and painted plywood planks nailed up horizontally around us. Despite the absence of fruitful soil, and the prevalence of pinched pockets, my family of thread-bare Greeks churned merrily from day to day as though each of us possessed a bank deposit book with lots of black numerals imprinted inside.

Primarily we were able to get along under this pervasive

delusion because our rickety wooden kitchen table was oft-times laden with a diverse spread of edibles. These victuals could not be characterized as *gourmet* entrees, certainly, but they were nutritionally sufficient to whisk me out the door to Public School #82 where my grade school pedagogue, Mr. Jonquil, was teaching me how to divide, multiply, and subtract numbers which I would never have much use for later in life; groceries that were nutritionally capable of carrying by subway my hollow-bellied mother to her daily scrambling as a waitress at the Piccadilly Coffee Shop in Manhattan; and to propel Cousin Peter up the steep sledding hill to High School #117 to take his place through text book pages in the damp jungles of Vietnam; and with more than enough energy left over to carry Christos (his parents had had the audacity to name him after Jesus Christ) to the Acropolis Cafeteria where, before it went out of business, he smeared wads of egg salad, tuna fish, peanut butter, and feta cheese between slices of white bread. (Christos was not an official member of my tribe, but Ya-Ya had taken him in off the streets because her daughter, Harriet, had treated him so shabbily.)

This same source of energy was most prominently responsible for carting my Ya-Ya on a growling city line bus to the dank-smelling kitchens of Jamaica Hospital; here she was engaged as an egg-scrambler, chicken-skinner, vegetable boiler, potato masher, carrot shaver, garlic chopper. Deep within her less-than five-foot, bone-revealing frame this proud Greek matron was tough as steel subway tracks; at the same time, she was the most gentle arbiter of family squabbles, performing this sacred duty rather like an Athenian goddess in her craggy Greek accent.

Half an hour after resolving one family shouting match or another, Ya-Ya would thump into the potato-peeling, cabbage-boiling, fish-stinking, dish-washing kitchens housed within that rusty stack of bricks; here, after knotting her canvas apron around her waist, she would stir and fry and broil and bake a dietitian's menu of foodstuffs for those suffering in the compartments on the floors above. Largely it was because my Ya-Ya had labored steadfastly for so many years in those stinking kitchens that my family always had more than enough meat to reheat and slap onto our plates at dinner time.

A generous, resourceful provider, Ya-Ya, under the umbrella of family love which she brandished readily, would take it upon herself to tuck a chicken leg or two into her purse during work hours, or slip three or four meatballs under her baggy cable-knit sweater—a sagging garment knitted by her own vein-laced claws; or, around Christmas or Easter, pilfer a petite steak or fleshy pork chop which she would stash somewhere on her person—quite possibly in what must've been blowzy bloomers.

Yes, it was first and foremost because of Ya-Ya's slyly executed largess that the family always had enough to chew on and, in addition, which shielded us from the preposterous notion that we were among the poorest of the poor in Jamaica, Queens. Miscellaneous fathers and mothers who inhabited the windward-leaning houses along our street were noticeably better off than us, holding regular jobs at Walgreens or H & R Block or Family Dollar or Sherwood's Garage, with several of them claiming ownership of a rusted Ford or dented Plymouth. In our household at the time we didn't possess so much as a bicycle (with or without a flat tire)—for us it was head out to school or work or the stores with holes in our shoes, or ride the subway or bus if we could scrape together enough coins for the fare.

* * *

On the heels of this woebegone legacy, all of us skittered from day to night on "a wing and a prayer," as they used to say after the big war. Throughout those years we dragged our close-to-the-bone bodies here and there without ever considering the mean straits within which we clambered. I slept on a folding cot in a corner of Stavros' and Christos' bedroom, second largest walled-in space in our humbling hacienda. Some nights when I sank onto the cot assigned to me it would snap closed and wrap its metal sidebars around my ribs until I could claw my way out into breathable air again.

As the leader of our immigrant hierarchy, Ya-Ya pitted prunes at the hospital, knitted blankets at home, played bingo at St. Demetrius, and slept in the largest room in our compact quarters; because there weren't enough beds to go around, she shared hers with one of Harriet's brood, Cousin Peter. (In later years I sometimes wondered if snuggling up close to the family's grand matriarch, night after night, was the reason he ended up being a committed member of the gay fraternity, going so far one spring as to march in a parade of like-minded souls in Greenwich Village. But I'm probably oversimplifying the business of how people choose to live their lives.)

My mother was a frail fluff of a sparrow—indeed, most members of our household (except for my pop) fell well short of standard American heft and stature. She did what little sleeping she could manage under a washed bare, loosely threaded quilt (purchased for three dollars from the Salvation Army) on the sunken-bottom couch in our living room, the smallest framed enclosure under those disintegrating shingles. Yet I never once heard her gripe about the rudeness of her sleeping accommodations, never a word about the aches she must've been nursing as she dozed on that hard, lumpy surface. I suppose my mapou was simply grateful to have a pillow to lay her head upon after distancing herself from my father's love affair with the bottle: a romance he was acting out most recently in a grim basement hideout in the Bronx.

Over and above Ya-Ya's munificence, every so seldom— usually at the end of a day in which my mother had collected a kerchief-full of tips at the Piccadilly, she would stop on her way home at Martell's, a popular "thirst-quenching bar and grill" in our neighborhood. Seated on a stool at the bar, so said Uncle Stavros, she would treat herself to a single martini, its green olive drowning at the bottom—a touch of "fancy living" no doubt intended to brighten her gloomy prospects.

While sipping her drink ever so slowly to make it last, she would gab about this and that with the bartender—she was very lonely in those days—before ordering a take-out brown paper bag full of the most delicious hot dogs ever roasted across the seven continents, each tucked into a golden brown bun. Tripping home, she would burst into our apartment with her arms wrapped around this still-warm bag of doggies, proclaiming proudly that she'd brought dinner home for "every last Greek on the block"—meaning the Hestiakos/Dropoulos crowd since we were the only Greeks embedded in that line up of wilted shelters.

Every one of us always-ravenous Mediterraneans would beam with gratitude over these spontaneous feasts staged by Mother Evangelina; joyfully we would smear the dogs with mustard, topping them with sauerkraut scooped out of a paper cup, before swallowing them in a couple of bites. Only fifteen minutes we needed to make a dozen dogs, and collateral fixings, disappear into Jamaica's dust-clotted humidity. Those hotties were so scrumptious we could barely speak after devouring the bag of them. After which we would sit glowing quietly around the kitchen table, ogling each other in self-satisfied contentment. Even as I think about those weiners these many years later I can taste their garlic-impregnated, 100% beef on my salivating tongue. Those hot dog parties staged by my benevolent mapou were yet another reason we'd been able to remain shielded from the knowledge that we were pathetically poor.

Once or twice Cousin Henry participated in these festivities, having wandered into our house unexpectedly at just the right moment—almost as if he could smell those grilled doggies from a mile away, where he was sharing two rooms up against the BMT tracks with his Aunt Harriet. My aunt was never invited to these hot dog feasts, nor did she ever show up for them unannounced. That's because Ya-Ya would never have opened the door to her. Why? Because Harriet, her fickle daughter, had married or at least aligned herself with six or seven pitiable males—nearly all of them not Greek, and then had abandoned each of them for reasons which, to my grand-mapou, were entirely unforgivable.

Being the family's principal wage earner, my self-proclaimed uncle, Christos, would contribute a box of kindness to the family larder from time to time as well, carrying into our apartment a cardboard carton packed with canned Chef Boyardee Raviolis, Heinz Baked Beans with onions, Bumble Bee Tuna, Hormel's Chili with kidney beans, and more. All plucked from the shelves of the Acropolis Cafeteria in which, it was rumored, he'd invested all of his savings. Occasionally he would add an exotic touch to our menu: a can of Dole's Pineapple chunks or, once, a whole hairy coconut. (The milky juice at its core was a special treat, each of us sipping a taste off the tip of a spoon.) Admittedly the unpredictable mix in Christos' occasional food banks sometimes resulted in truly weird buffets: one night we dined on beef jerky smeared with Velveeta Cheese, mashed chick peas with a pinch of paprika, and iceberg lettuce drenched in vinegar. For dessert we plundered a three-day-old box of donut holes.

Because Uncle Stavros was a rather lazy handyman who, when he felt like it, fixed this and that for neighbors, nearby shops, and small service businesses, he never returned home after his labors with a bag of groceries, but he could be counted on to provide rubber washers, two-inch nails, Draino, assorted screws, a jar of Elmer's glue to stop leaks in our faucets, to stifle the wind at our windows, to keep drains draining, and the toilet flushing. Stavros's here-and-there work schedule meant he was around the house more than anyone else, and every time one of us turned around, he or she would smack into him—especially because our living space was much too small for six eating, drinking, sleeping, swearing human beings.

* * *

The primary psychological reason my family never fully accepted we were fretfully poor, I think, was that we could actually *see* "the other side of the tracks" from our side of the tracks. It was set at the far end of a yellowy lighted concrete tunnel under an overpass of the Long Island Railroad. At the other end of this tunnel we could observe at different times a pile of tread-worn automobile tires, flattened wooden fruit boxes, smashed beer bottles, a supermarket shopping cart with no wheels, maybe a dead cat or dog. In the minds of us kids, this collection of junk added up to the "poor side of town."

Not too often some of the neighborhood brats—brashly we called ourselves "alley rats"—would creep into the overhanging arch so we could listen to a train rumbling overhead. Or maybe to look around for anything that might come in handy to a bunch of empty-handed goats. If truth be told, we never found anything worth carrying back home—a bicycle tire on a bent rim, a carton of water-logged newspapers, an unrolled condom and, most chilling of all, a foot-long, rusty-bladed kitchen knife that Ricky, Mike, and I were certain was stained with blood. That discovery sent the three of us scuttling back out into the sunlight, dashing home to the safety of our nests.

Still another reason it never quite dawned on my family that we were so grasping poor was that we always had oodles of entertainment to amuse us. The recreational phase of our lives got started the night Cousin Henry (who believed working for someone else was "the dumbest thing any jerk could do") barged into our apartment with a plastic box clamped under his arm: turned out to be a beat up old radio. Two round red knobs were stuck on its face like eyeballs in a clown's head. And once he plugged it into the wall and clicked one of those knobs, we heard a man's voice wailing robustly inside the box, "You Ain't Nothing But a Hound Dog!"

What we never figured out was how Henry, who rarely had more than two-bits in his pocket, had managed to lay his hands on this magic box. Curiously, in less than a month, with that radio playing day and night, the songs we heard squawking out of the box began working their way into our heads. Before long Christos started singing along with these ditties. Then Uncle Stavros began picking up the tunes, singing from the bottom of his lungs. Pretty soon I found myself joining in too. Quite the Greek chorus we made! This awful noise went on for several months, and it didn't stop until Ya-Ya griped sharply that we didn't have enough money to pay our electric bill.

Because we lived a block away from Jamaica Arena, we also enjoyed plenty of *live* entertainment. The back wall of the arena was a thin sheet of tin, painted brown, and several of us alley rats, along with a couple of sports-loving grown-ups, punched holes in the tin wall with a hammer slammed against an iron nail. Over time, we stretched these punctures wider so we could see more of the action inside, and without having to squint so much.

On Friday nights we'd witness match ups between young white, black, and Latin boxers. I guess the fighters who were still standing after six rounds must've been handed a fistful of the bucks the arena had collected from ticket sales. Since there wasn't much money floating around our neighborhood, these sluggers fought like crazy devils to pick up a share of the take: very entertaining! Peeking through that hole in the wall made my eyes sore, but the bloody lips—and one night I saw a nose hanging half off the fighter's face—made up for the eye strain.

* * *

Probably the biggest reason we never gripped the shoulders of our poverty with both hands was that beautiful figurine of the Holy Mother which my family possessed. Maybe six inches tall and made of what my mother called "hand-cut crystal," you could see straight through to its other side. With its narrow base, it would've been easy to knock over and break, so it was never allowed to come out from behind that pane of glass in the cabinet. But this didn't stop me from reaching inside from time to time to slide my fingertips over its glossy surface—cold and slippery as ice.

Thinking about that statuette years later, I realized the Holy Mother had provided my family with a sense that, no matter what fate tossed at our feet, everything would work out just fine. Probably we felt this way because we all believed (without a pinch of proof) that this figurine was extremely valuable—worth hundreds of U.S. bucks. Maybe more. And that if the rent, electric, and gas bills ever started stacking up on our kitchen table, or if Ya-Ya should ever get caught pocketing a couple of sausages from the hospital, Uncle Stavros would wrap the Holy Mother in a sheet of newspaper and walk it up to Dinty's Pawn Shop. There he'd trade it in for a pocketful of greenbacks.

Even during that stretch of time—maybe half a year though it seemed much longer—when Stavros would scissor little squares out of his newspaper so we could wipe our behinds, no one in my family ever bothered even to hint at or joke about our being poor as mice living off crumbs of communion bread at St. Demetrius. We tip-toed from day to day without paying any attention to the fact that no one in the family had a bank book with his name imprinted inside.

Grandpapou Yiannis had his own special way of avoiding thinking about our empty purses: He established a personal dream to see the Old Country once more before he died. The true motivation behind this goal, if you ask me, was that by returning to Fidakia, the village of his birth, he'd be able to escape Ya-Ya's wrath, byproduct of a long-standing, mysterious feud between them. Sailing to Greece was all he ever talked about! As a part-time superintendent for a broken down walk up in Brooklyn, however, we knew all along he'd never be able to put aside enough cash to board a freighter clutching a cloth sack packed with his belongings. Ultimately what he really wanted, we came to believe, was to be buried in the Old Country's dusty soil. Poor grandpapou—he died in an ambulance on a Brooklyn highway before he could realize his pipe dream.

* * *

Whatever pennies and nickels trickled into my pockets came from running errands for the McQuinns, the family living up the stairs from us. Here and there Mrs. McQuinn, known in the neighborhood as Mrs. Queenie, and once in a bloody moon Mr. McQuinn, whom we tagged as The Quiet Man, would ask me to run up to Charlie's Grocery to pick up a loaf of bread, a quart of milk, a bottle of beer. (If you had the money, Charlie would sell beer to anyone, including half-pint kids.) Or it might be a hike to Walgreen's to buy a jar of Vicks VapoRub for Ricky—their eleven-year-old always seemed to be dribbling at the nose. One time I had to scuff in my ratty sneakers all the way to Marco's Pet Store to buy a gold fish for their nine-year-old daughter, Millie. (Shortly after I delivered the fish in a plastic bag filled with water, she named it Goldilocks.)

The coins that were dropped into my hand to do these errands were immediately handed over to Mr. Epstein in his candy shop under the BMT tracks. In Eppy's a kid could load his pockets with sweets for fifteen, maybe eighteen cents—the candyman sold licorice balls for two cents each, lumps of raspberry jelly coated with chocolate for three cents, plus candy-dotted strips of paper at the "highway robbery" price of five cents per sheet. Fondling the bulge of candy treats in my pocket made me feel as though I was truly wealthy.

The sad ending to my candy-driven riches happened one Saturday when Millie McQuinn was visiting a classmate on the next block: The gold fish I'd carried home for Mrs. Queenie had ended up floating instead of swishing around in its bowl. Millie's mom was so upset over the passing of Goldilocks that she scrambled down the stairs to our apartment—something she only did around the Christmas holiday, asking, actually begging me to "hop over to the pet store" and buy a new goldfish before her little girl returned home.

This happened on a gray, wet, chilly day when I was feeling kind of blue, so I was unable to stop myself from saying to Mrs. Queenie, "I don't feel like going to the pet store."

"Why the hell not?" she demanded.

"Cause I'm too busy today." Busy my foot—at that moment, I was just feeling plain selfish, in no mood to help anyone but myself.

Queenie McQuinn was stunned. "You telling me you won't do this one little favor for me?" which meant, *after all the coins I've slipped into your hand.* Meanly I shook my head left and right, and the woman with burning red eyes shrieked, called me a "selfish little son of a bitch," and then tears began squirting out of her eyes.

Mrs. Queenie thundered out of our apartment and scaled the stairs as quickly as a fireman going up a ladder to put out a fire, shouting all the way that I was a "freakin' selfish brat." Instantly this incident had shut down my only source of income. Thinking about what happened that day, I was never able to figure out why I'd refused to go to the pet shop for her—I liked going to the pet shop so I could pet a dog or two. Nor did I understand why I'd done this to poor little Millie, who was a nice kid. Surely Millie, like her mom, must have cried the eyeballs right out of her sockets when she learned Goldilocks had been flushed down the toilet.

* * *

Once I'd lost that steady (if irregular) source of income I began keeping my eyes peeled for alternative fiscal opportunities, and fate came to my rescue a short time later. I woke up very early one Sunday morning, crawled off my cot, crept into the bathroom to pee. Lying on top of the toilet tank, as if waiting for me in particular, were three crumpled dollar bills and a scattering of coins. I realized immediately that my Uncle Stavros had stayed out late on Saturday night, downing a few too many brews at Martell's. After bragging about how much liquor Dionysus could hold with a local tippler—or some such boast, my uncle had wobbled home. Wavering half drunk in our bathroom, he'd emptied his pockets on the toilet tank, crawled out of his clothes, hauled his beer-bloated belly into our shared bedroom, and fell away into an alcohol-induced sleep.

With everyone still knocked out in their beds that morning, I stood stiff as an icicle a long while in front of the toilet, staring at the money. And once I'd finished doing my business, I extended my arm over the toilet tank and my fingers, as if they were attached to someone else's hand, scooped up a quarter, a dime, three pennies, along with a wrinkled one-dollar bill. Hastily I stashed this red-hot cash into the pocket of my pajamas. It had been so easy to transfer my uncle's riches from the toilet tank onto my side of the ledger that I never for a moment felt I'd done anything wrong.

I figured that this deposit into my make-believe bank account, if spent just a few coins at a time, would last me many months, extending the period of my discretionary wealth far beyond anything I'd ever dreamed possible. In addition to malted milk balls, bubble gum, and Tootsie Rolls at Eppy's, I might even treat myself to a personal luxury, such as one of those twenty-nine cent, lighter-than-air balsam airplanes which came in a build-it-yourself kit. Once pieced together, a thrust of the arm could send such a craft soaring a dozen feet from where you stood—amazing!

Eventually it was the acquisition of that hand-propelled craft which led to my family finding out I'd stolen money from my Uncle Stavros. Christos, the most alert one in our bunch, noticed me forcing the wing into the main stem of balsam in our bedroom and asked me flat out how I'd gotten hold of such a "sleek hunk of aviation." Stammering, I was unable to make up a story quick enough that I thought he might believe. Christos read the guilt on my face right off and, just like a big baby, I burst out into a wash of tears.

Gratefully the family's disappointment in me passed after several months, and they began to trust me again. Ashamed to admit, however, after squandering all of my cash reserves, I found myself doing the same thing again—stealing, only this time it was from Riggles Five 'N Dime on upper Jamaica Avenue. This time it wasn't money to buy sweets that I stole: I dropped into my pants pocket a miniature yo-yo (yellow and green) which, I learned later, clicked pleasantly when you swung it toward the ground. The strange thing about this theft was that I'd received a perfectly good yo-yo as a birthday gift a couple months earlier.

* * *

Happy to report now that, after the yo-yo caper, I never again stockpiled my wealth by taking what belonged to somebody else. Time skipped along in a kind of tap dancing rhythm, and I eventually became what Cousin Henry liked to call "a working jackass." I began delivering groceries for Charlie's Grocery on a regular basis, and this enabled me to purchase all the jelly beans a young fellow could desire: the black licorice-flavored beans were my favorite.

The most exciting aspect of this new money-making venture was that I got to peddle Charlie's bicycle, with its shiny handlebars, red fenders, and wide metal basket, all around the neighborhood. I delivered bread, milk, cheese, cabbage, and similar delectibles to the homes of local families. Most of the customers I delivered goods to were wrapped in loose layers of crinkled skin. In addition to the dollar Charley paid to me for each delivery I made, many of his crotchety customers dropped a few coins into my hand as a tip.

During this period of financial expansion, I learned that Cousin Henry had given up on his life-long ambition of never holding a job: He became what Stavros told me was a "sales representative," visiting small shops in the area. (It wasn't until much later I learned what he was doing to those small business owners.) After another year or two had frittered away into the air-borne dust of Queens, and I'd finished wrestling with math, history, and English in high school, I too took on a full-time job—as a clerk in Crumbs Bakery. In addition to cash on the counter twice-a-month, I was encouraged to take home a bag of day-old donuts, bagels, or rolls whenever they baked more than they could sell.

It was around this period in my history of rags to riches that Christos gave up on the idea of marrying his beloved, much-married Harriet, and began hanging out with Euthalia Damocles. They went to the movies, out for walks on summer evenings, and only God knows what else they got around to doing with each other. Before any of us were paying close attention, Christos had moved out from under our roof, taking his scraggly beard and pickle jar full of coins with him. Three months later he traipsed down the aisle gripping Euthalia's hand at St. Demetrius. What a surprise it was to us—we'd always figured if Christos couldn't have Aunt Harriet, he wouldn't have any woman. This development left the family one salary poorer than we'd been prior to Christos having had the audacity to fall in love.

Even though I was now bringing home a fistful of cash

twice a month, the loss of Christos's fatter purse meant there was less to go around. At the same time, as Ya-Ya pointed out, there was one less mouth to feed. But the bones of my dear Greek matron were showing more and more through her arms and legs, and she seemed more and more weary after a day in the hospital's clammy kitchens, so I had no doubt it was getting much harder for her to slip a lamb chop into her pocketbook.

Now, as I stand at the bottom line of this accounting of my family's financial history, I think it's fair to say everything worked out fine and dandy for us, just the way our never-say-die hearts always imagined it would. And this came about even without a helping hand from the statuette of the Holy Mother. For the first time in years of turning our backs on the creaking poverty that'd been hounding my family, I was able to state openly, and rather proudly, that the Hestiakos/Dropoulos crowd had been bottom-of-the-barrel poor for all those many years. And yet somehow—by the grace of God, we had worked our way through these "dirt poor" conditions without leaving too many scars on our souls. Why? Somewhere along the way it must've dawned on us that it really didn't matter if our pockets were empty as long as we were members of a loving family. For as long as these mothers and fathers, grandparents, cousins, uncles, and hangers-on were always at your side when you faltered on the cracked pavement of life, you were rich as Croesus.

Ya-Ya's Declaration
of Independence

For half a dozen years, maybe more, my family stood out in tight shoes and loose collars one day every spring to witness the strutting and streaming and boom-boom-booming of paraders along Fifth Avenue—head-on into the blade of an icy north-westerly, with the blue-and-white striped banners of the Old Country flapping in the lead, and the coffee-grinds-and-ketchup smudged Department of Sanitation trucks sweeping up the hot dog wrappers and manure to the rear. All in honor of the long-lost, never-heard-of heroes of Greece's battles for independence from the Turks. Each member of my family would flush with pride over the rousing martial appeal to a nationalism that didn't make much sense at the feet of Manhattan's skyscrapers. But that amusement, that passion has been lost to us forever. If the truth be told, my grandmother on my mother's side, known to us affectionately as Ya-Ya Hysterical, who loved a parade as much as those she'd taught to love a parade, behaved in such a manner that final year of our attendance as to make it unseemly for any of us to show our faces ever again on the occasion of so much public pomp.

* * *

A woman of seventy or more years should be forbidden by an act of Congress to wear a bikini bathing suit—especially at a parade attracting thousands of witnesses. At least that's what Ya-Ya's daughters, Delphinia and Evangelina and Merrula, were surely thinking at curb's edge as they stared not at the naked sticks of their mother's arms and legs but at the stockinged calves of the swaying military men in white skirts and maroon vests and fez caps. Among the spectators it was just the opposite: The smooth young faces, even the sagging middle-aged faces, were aimed not at the handsome soldiers strutting by but at the old woman in the bikini on the sidelines; she was wiggling in time with the marching music. Crusty vultures in black, capelike dresses could be seen fingering their worry beads at an alarming rate, as if gazing upon the devil incarnate since it was widely accepted among my kind that the devil could assume any number of disguises.

At last the daughters could hold out no longer.

"Are you trying to disgrace us?" Merrula demanded, biting her nails as she spoke.

"I never been ashamed of my body."

"Are you trying to get arrested?" moaned Delphinia, scanning the crowds nervously to see if a cop was within handcuffing distance.

"America's a free country."

Peering intensely at the row of rifles passing in parade, as if she'd like to get hold of one and lead Ya-Ya away at gunpoint, my mother screeched: "Are you trying to catch a cold?"

Ya-Ya's shrill cry went right up my spine: "Foolish child: Must be 95 degrees out here!"

"Where'd you get that . . . thing . . . anyway?" said Delphinia, sneering at her mother's costume.

"Macy's," Ya-Ya declared. "On sale!"

As far as the men were concerned, this was the women's problem. My father Alexandros Sr.—prior to his recent drunken spree—and my mother's brother Stavros and Merrula's husband Kosmas, all veterans of foreign wars—or so they claimed, had driven over the Brooklyn Bridge to enjoy an afternoon of military pageantry: Nothing was going to get in the way of their opportunity to indulge in war-time nostalgia, a pastime apparently understood only by those who'd carried weapons into battle.

One of them said: "Imagine if we'd had to fight the war in white skirts!"

Another said: "Great day to bear the colors."

The last, a realist, added: "Yeah, but it's kinda hot for spring so maybe skirts are not such a bad idea."

Just a little kid at the time, I'm able to pass this story on mostly from the different versions I've heard over the years, being too short at the time to see as much as I would've liked. But there had indeed been a gush of mid-summer weather that month, and the family had been led by our conditioning against the windy lions of March, early that morning, to wrap ourselves in woolens instead of cottons. So Ya-Ya was perfectly comfortable while we were sweaty and sticky and generally miserable due partly to the thermometer but mostly to my grandmother's public demonstration.

"Don't you feel any shame?" Delphinia inquired.

"It's my name-day," Ya-Ya explained. "On my name-day I do anything I want."

Unable to avoid overhearing them even in all that crowd noise, Uncle Stavros mumbled to his comrades-at-arms, "God save us from old women."

* * *

Later on Merrula theorized that Ya-Ya had shown up in that teeny weeny bikini to get back at her husband—a devil-may-care response to a red-hot argument they'd had that morning over no-one-knew-what. My aunt may have been right, for my grandpapou, to our knowledge, had not shown his face on Fifth Avenue that year though he admired a parade as well as any Hestiakos.

My father ascribed the agonizing display of barely covered, crumpled flesh—agonizing because it was too powerful a reminder of his own perishability, I suppose—to the old gal having gone "off her noodle," adding with a snicker: "She's practicing for the bathing beauty contest at Coney Island." Considering my mother's agitated state, that statement amounted to an act of bravery.

Kosmas had his own theory and, as an in-law, made the mistake of expressing it: "Just going through a second childhood, so let her be."

The eyes of all three sisters grew large at this hint that their mother may have been going senile, and it was pointed out to him by his sister-in-law, Delphinia, that senility had never had taken much of a hold on their hard, Hestiakos skulls. "All of us will be in our graves," she insisted, her chin jutting, "before it comes to that."

Probably the truth was a lot more obvious than any of them figured. Having spent so many years putting aside her own impulses—to satisfy parents, priests, husband, children, sisters and brother, not to mention grocers and cleaning girls and passengers in her cab, now that she was past seventy Ya-Ya could well have dropped her skin and bones into a bikini on the premise that she'd finally grown up enough to do precisely what she damn well pleased when she damn well pleased where she damn well pleased.

Whatever the true reason, Ya-Ya had resisted all attempts to be driven to the parade. "It's no trouble to pick you up in the car, mama," her daughters had offered a third time. "Are you deaf or jess stupid?" she'd screeched. "I said I meet you at the parade." And meet us she did: pulled off her raincoat and there she was—all ninety, shrunken pounds of her in two strips of silvery cloth, more like a pair of band-aids than a bathing suit. The family was so shocked they turned to stone just long enough to give her a foothold in the day's fanfare.

Ya-Ya's more-than-half-naked appearance did have one positive side-effect: Except for my father, my family is quite short, even for Greeks, so we often missed seeing a lot of the parade, but as soon as my grandmother unveiled, people jumped out of her way and let all of us walk right up to the police barrier. For the first time in years even a shrimp like me got to see a few of the polished faces of the kids dragging their feet behind the religion classes' banner, and the knot-like knees of the dandy chestnut horses, and the baton-twirling high school girls kicking their naked legs high. On the other hand we were also much easier to be seen, standing at the police barrier, and the Hestiakos adults didn't much care for the looks they were getting from surrounding witnesses—especially from one well-rounded figure in a dark blue uniform: A cop had taken up a position on the other side of the Avenue, legs wide apart to maintain his balance, thumbs notched in his belt with an air of self-importance. Once he caught sight of Ya-Ya, however, his hands dropped to his side and he took to staring at the old woman intensely, as if trying to figure out if she was in violation of one ordinance or other. Then he started casting his eyes over those who surrounded her—obviously the family, trying to figure out why we didn't do something about her so he wouldn't have to do something about her. It would seem avoidance is sometimes the best way to solve a problem be- cause the officer marched in step with the Women's Hellenic League and parked his belly a block or two away.

* * *

The Greek community of New York City seems as homoge- neous as a tiny hamlet on the island of Melos: No matter where we go in the boroughs, we bump into olive-oil skinned com- patriots of our acquaintance. So it was no surprise when we spotted Mrs. Cyclethes of Jamaica, Queens, which is where my mother and several members of the family had moved into a two-family frame house, after losing my grandparents' house in Brooklyn. Mrs. Cyclethes was a walking broom whose sole purpose in life was to sweep up some dirt on someone every day; one look at Ya-Ya and she had filled her quota for a month. Sighting the cynical gleam of Mrs. Cyclethes' plum-sized eyes aimed at her family, Evangelina immediately tossed the rain coat over her mother's shoulders. But Ya-Ya slipped out from under it, bent low, and chicken-stepped under the police barrier where her daughters couldn't get their hands on her—not without exposing themselves to humiliating laughter.

The clergy and elders of St. Demetrius came marching along solemnly behind a silky purple streamer which proclaimed their allegiance to the Orthodox faith. Out into the middle of the street Ya-Ya hopped, joining their loose formation not ten feet behind Father Nick. Glancing over his shoulder, he shivered as if he'd been struck by lightning, his ears smoking like the Camels' cigarette sign on Broadway. From behind, church elders stared fiercely at Ya-Ya's road-map legs, the meatless ribs poking out of her back. Soon an astonished, low-keyed murmur spiraled out of the rows of bystanders on both sides of the street, and they began waving their tiny blue-and-white flags furiously, joyfully at Ya-Ya. You would've thought she'd just liberated Paris.

* * *

Father Nicholas was a liberal-minded soul. His speech was laced with American expressions, and he sometimes held up two fingers as a symbol of peace, the way "flower children" used to do in the 60s. Using a hammered out chin and thick black brush under his nose to advantage, he had managed to draw women into a more active role in the parish. Watching him get around the women to do his bidding, the men in my family had expressed the opinion on numerous occasions that he had seen "a thing or two of life" before he had dressed in black. Yet he was unable to see the lighter side of an aged, not particularly well-preserved parishioner in a bikini marching close behind him on Manhattan's most elegant avenue, especially as they paraded a block away from the sand castle spires of St. Patrick's Cathedral and its adjacent, imposing parish house. For one panicky moment the good Father must've choked at the thought that the Cardinal might be watching through the gauzy curtains of his Catholic chambers, wondering what to make of Greek Orthodoxy as that ancient, practically naked servant of God marched just to the rear of the brass cross borne by the man in black.

Of even larger concern to Father Nick, I imagine, is that St. Demetrius' delegation was only a block removed from the reviewing stand, where His Eminence, The Most Holy Bishop of Athens, Iakovaros, in town especially for this grand marshalling of dwarfed flags and overblown trumpets, was presiding. Youngish Nick couldn't very well turn around and begin lambasting this bony, diminutive member of his flock—it might look like he was bullying an old lady. Plus it would throw blocks of paraders out of step. Probably thinking the heat had softened her brain, he played it safe, trying to ignore her—no doubt praying hard that she would just fade back into the crowd and disappear from sight and, therefore, from mind.

As Ya-Ya marched ahead, catching up to him, her sandals began clipping Father Nick's heels, and with laughter sweeping through rows of a new section of witnesses like a brush fire, the women in my family—yanking me by the hand—ducked under the police barrier and tramped alongside the marchers in the parade. Reluctantly the men of the family followed us under the barriers; they had no choice if they didn't want to lose sight of us. Our spiritual leader spotted my clan. Even at that distance, it was obvious Father Nick was flushed from his chin to the roots of his hair. He kept jerking his head toward us, trying to get one of us to come over and do something. Even if my family had been willing to claim her as their own, Ya-Ya wouldn't have listened to them; she would only have gotten riled up, and who knows what she might've done once her blood got boiling. Besides, as Uncle Kosmas had mentioned, what harm was she doing? The best my family could do was stay close enough to her so that when she got tired of the joke, or of putting her grand vanity on public display, or whatever it was to her, they could throw the raincoat over her bones and hustle her off like a movie star after a world premiere.

* * *

Approaching Central Park, I remember seeing the august reviewing stand: all but two were male, mostly in dark suits, and all standing, all still, all grave, and not one smile on any of their faces. As we moved within range of their viewing perspective, Father Nick couldn't hold back any longer. He stopped and spun around, raised the polished cross into the air—as if to ward off Dracula, and blurted something to Ya-Ya. I wish I could report which words had sprung out of his jaws, maybe something like, "You are embarrassing yourself, your family, and your church!" Or had he forgotten himself and leveled a string of blasphemies at her. But I did get an eyeful of the comic situation: a mere boy in his thirties, dressed up to his neck in black, attempting to admonish someone twice his age, nearly half his height, dressed from her neck to her ankles in ragged skin. Unmoved by his appeal, his gesticulations, his bright red ears, Ya-Ya marched around Father Nick who, astonished into immobility, was soon passed up by the entire St. Demetrius congregation. Ya-Ya was now leading our parish, and she began to kick her knees and wave her hands at the crowds like a drum majorette. They waved back gleefully.

"Will you look at her," cried Delphinia, "just look at her!"

"Don't make me look!" hollered Evangelina, unable not to look.

"I could just die," exclaimed Merrula.

"What the hell," said Stavros, trying to justify his inaction, "she's just having a good time."

Kosmas laughed heartily, stopping only when Merrula pointed her small gray eyes into her husband's big ochre eyes.

* * *

A junior high school band from Staten Island stalled near the reviewing stand to play a jazzed-up version of one of the Greek national anthems, which had been subject to change several times under new regimes. The honks and shrieks and crashes of their saxes and clarinets and cymbals were hardly noticed by the bystanders, however. All eyes and ears on the reviewing stand had swiveled toward a four-foot eleven inch sack of bones, who was swinging both arms over her head at all that mighty austerity, which included a sprinkling of Irish, Italian, Polish, and Puerto Rican city fathers looking to get their pictures in the papers. The public and religious emissaries writhed in their places, but I did notice a few smiles breaking into their faces. Except for that of the Most Holy Iakovaros, his slate-colored, frozen facade seemingly held up by the knotted, wiry, massive silver beard resting on his broad chest.

With one eye on Iakovaros, Father Nick approached Ya-Ya again, inspiring her to break out of the line of marchers and start strutting in the direction of His Holiness and His Almost Honor, the Deputy Mayor. If Ya-Ya wasn't crazy, then you would've had to think she'd been guzzling metaxa and/ or ouzou since dawn; that's one combo, they tell me, that could send anyone's brain into a tail spin. But I don't believe my grandmapou had relied on alcoholic beverages to free her inhibitions. Rather she was drunk on her own audacity, I suspect, like a person accepting an award who, captivated by the sound of her own voice, could no longer tell she was making an immortal ass of herself.

* * *

It was becoming clearer with every kick of the leg, every wave of the hand that my family would have to claim her as their own, risking profound humiliation, along with her wrath, for the greater good of making things right between America and Greece. Before they could undertake such a delicate mission, however, a pair of policemen on horseback—they were, after all, under the scrutiny of the Assistant Chief of Police on the reviewing stand—felt obliged to overcome their wariness and approach the old bag. Seeing they meant to prevent her from shaking hands with the Bishop, Ya-Ya cut loose with so high-pitched a yelp that one of the sleek chocolate horses bucked into the sunlight, raising its front hoofs like a show horse, and this caused the other horse to give in to the same impulse.

This part remains vivid in my mind: The crowds roared with fright and delight, and began to disintegrate into a swaying, jumping, swarming, swinging fragmentation of humanity. Waves of hollering and pushing and running and neighing overwhelmed us. Then I lost hold of my mother's hand. The stampede swelled against the wooden barriers, knocking them over, and the parade joined the crowds and the crowds joined the parade. People were running in circles. People were screaming and shouting. People were chortling and crying. I could hear my mother calling out, "Alex! Alexandros!" But I couldn't see her. What I did catch a glimpse of was Bishop Iakovaros standing rigidly, his arms outstretched as if offering a benediction, or maybe he was walking in his sleep and thought he was having a nightmare.

* * *

It was all over in minutes, and the most grievous results seemed to be some toppled hairdos and lost false teeth and a bent trombone and a trampled toy Greek soldier and a hot dog or two that had squirted out of their buns. A couple of balloons had been relinquished to the sky as well, sailing over our heads in a light-headed, fantastic dance. Looking back on that miniature riot, I saw it not as ugly so much as joyful: An audacious, skin-and-bones gramapou, emboldened by her seven-tenths of a century on earth, had enabled the city to unite in a spirit of celebration, not that of Greek Independence but of human freedom—celebrating for no other reason than that we were alive.

In the confusion the hands of Evangelina and Stavros wrenched Ya-Ya out of the hands of the mob, which seemed to have claimed her as their own, possibly in gratitude for the life-force she had released into the day. Swiftly my family bundled her in the raincoat and separated her from the crowds, finding no struggle left in her by this time. Leaving her in Evangelina's hands, seated on a bench outside Central Park, Stavros went off to scout up the rest of the family. Soon the Hestiakos gang had been reunited, and they escorted my grandmother down a side street in search of our cars. Despite too many cars parked legally and illegally on side streets, that yellow door on the driver's side of the Plymouth made ours easy to find. Then Kosmas and Merrula went off to find their own car, bright red and much newer, much faster than ours. Throughout the slow, ungainly process of squeezing our bodies into the car, Ya-Ya said not a word.

Along the narrow streets of Manhattan we bumped, rolling toward the Brooklyn Bridge. Strangely, my family didn't even mention the principal excitement of the day: Maybe they were afraid chastising Ya-Ya would set her off again. Glancing at my grandmother in the back seat, petite and white and subdued under the raincoat, surrounded by the dark hulks of Uncle Stavros and Aunt Delphinia, I couldn't help feeling sorry for her, as if the human spirit itself were under arrest. Just then, Ya-Ya winked at me.

Growing Up with the Evil Eye

Though they tell me a "hag with powers" gleamed into my carriage when I was six months old, the earliest recollection I have of The Evil Eye dates back to when I had reached the bright-eyed age of ten . . . a series of events which—in keeping with fate's wry, unpredictable temperament—had as its catalyst my father's passion for roasted red peppers. For if my mother hadn't led me into Charley's Grocery on Jamaica Avenue in search of shiny, bell-shaped vegetables, on our way home from St. Demetrius that Sunday morning, I might never have been stricken by the gaze of Mrs. Anna Rhinosos.

"Four red peppers—hard and fat," Mother Evangelina demanded, giving Charley the full Greek inflection since she believed sounding ethnic might save her a few pennies. (Mama sounded like she just came from the other side.) Except for a funeral in Chicago, as far as I know she'd never been out of New York State. Seems immigrant education can work in reverse. Instead of trying to Americanize her parents, Evangelina was so caught up in our heritage that she imitated the speech of my grandparents and their friends.

Dried out by routine and length of service, Charley revealed a secret tendon in his neck with every reach, setting the peppers one at a time into the tin bowl-shaped scale with care—no, with love, for food was less compromised by commerce in those days, and therefore was more respected by seller and buyer.

"So vat else?" said the proprietor, countering with his own brand of ethnicity, apparently in the belief that sounding ethnic might win him a few extra pennies of profit.

"Quarter pound butter," said she, "but don't sell me nothing more."

As Charley sealed the block of white butter in that thick, pearly grocery paper, into the store oozed Mrs. Rhinosos brandishing jowls that hung long enough to flap, and polka-dot eyes seemingly snipped from a child's drawing of a witch. A shedding green sack of a coat was stretched over her circular person, and a flat pink hat with a mashed paper lily was pinned to her hair—if not directly into her brain. The hapless creature was referred to as Mrs. in our neighborhood not in deference to her marital status but because she'd passionately desired all of her known life to be a member of that holy state: Not to gain the company of a man so much as the babies that might've resulted from such a connection.

With her remarkably bulbous body, and undeniable density of brain, and having given up speaking as a young woman—mostly out of habit, I suspect, since no one addressed her, she'd never to my knowledge been in danger of having her marital condition altered. Indeed it was said her portliness and thick-headedness were a direct result of a build up of too much unspent passion. Benevolently nature came to the rescue, gathering this pent-up energy into a strange power . . . or so it was widely held in that predominantly Greek neighborhood in Jamaica, a section of Queens that has been described cynically, if accurately, as a junkyard without a fence.

In the tradition of Hecate, the goddess of witchcraft, Mrs. Rhinosos used her special gifts for devilish ends: She hobbled about the borough aiming those pinpoint eyes at youngsters in an apparent attempt to extract the bloom from a child's face, the idea being, presumably, to improve her connubial opportunities by exchanging her own dour expressions for their pink, smiling cheeks. A second theory held that she wanted a child of her own so desperately she had taken to staring longingly into the eyes of youngsters since staring at men for thirty odd years had done her no good whatsoever. I lean toward the second theory, if only because I can't imagine why the Mrs. would've wanted to take custody of my bland brown eyes. Either way, Mrs. Rhinosos drifted straight at me that morning and slid her eyes over me "like a snake over grass," to quote my mother. Though I doubt she had actually witnessed that now-famous gaze, my mapou obviously had sensed it because she dropped the pepper—plop! on the floor, rolled around as if on skates and yanked my arm, and all that was attached to it, toward the door.

As we clattered out of that emporium of cans and jars and brown paper bags, Charley hollered, "Mrs. Dropolous, vat about your peppers—your budder?"

"Throw them in garbage, Charley," she cried, not looking back. "They're spoiled now!"

The grocer was unable to heed her advice not merely because he was a shrewd man of business; it was also because the door had already sprung shut, cutting him off from the timeless wisdom of Greece . . . diluted though it was by decades of making do in America. Besides, good grocer that he was, Charley would not have been able to work into his myth-consciousness the notion that a single glance from an old maid could turn butter sour, make eggs stink in their shells, dry the roots of snake plants, turn sugar green in the bowl, cause seeds in a red pepper to rot, and incite a mother to dash out of his store dragging her son after her. Being towed by the hand along the street, I was as mystified as Charley by Evangelina's hasty flight. That's because The Evil Eye was a subject Greeks avoided discussing around children, like Americans avoid discussing sex around their kids. When I breathlessly tried to ask if she had spotted mold on the butter, or a worm in a pepper, she yanked my ear lobe to shut me up. No big surprise:

Greek parents did not permit their off-spring to put in even one penny's worth of good sense.

Probably it was different for kids back in our glory days, The Golden Age of Greece. If they had been shut up, where would Western civilization be today? What would Plato and Aristotle and Socrates have done with all those ideas building up in their heads? Either developed enormous Evil Eyes, or simply exploded. Probably the decline of Greece began when parents started shutting up their kids. Now all that's left of those riches of the imagination is a protective attitude toward the children—a desire to save them from The Evil Eye, in essence, to shield them from knowledge itself.

Along the sidewalk we bounded like a pair of pink Spaulding high bouncers—the kind city kids used for playing stickball, and the escape reminded me of another retreat I'd been making—a mental escape from a mid-term math quiz that was lying in wait for me the next morning. An impending doom I had managed to block out of my mind for weeks. And breathing in the fragrance of tiny fresh leaves on Jamaica's valiant maples—popping out of their buds despite being surrounded by so much concrete, my mind swam out from the mysteries of mother and math into the warm waters of imagined, endless summer vacations at Rockaway Beach with its miles of yellow sand.

As soon as my mother had double locked the door of our house behind us, and had peeked out through the heavy brown drapes that stunk of incense and carbon dioxide, the hysteria she'd saved up like pennies in the sugar bowl spilled over: "Take everythin' off!" she shouted, and began unbuttoning my pants.

Having already embarked upon the age of modesty, I broke away from her and cried, "I can do it myself!" My mapou, restraining herself, stared at me with eyes that reminded me of what you see at the bottom of a kaleidoscope. When she took a step toward me, I began unbuttoning my shirt. But I did it too slowly for her, so she began yelling: "Fasta! Fasta! Fasta!" Each time I disconnected myself from a wad of cloth, she would grab the shirt, trousers, or socks out of my hands, turn each inside out, and proceed to tie it into knots. In minutes I stood before her in my underwear, perplexed and shy, wavering beside the made-in-Japan reproduction of a classic Greek vase on a pedestal . . . one of those ever-present reminders of a great past, as if Greeks everywhere were quietly conspiring to make a comeback.

"Hey *Vreh!*" my mother reiterated, "everythin'—off!"

"It's chilly," I complained.

"Off!" she threatened, "or else!" terrifying me with her vagueness.

Gripping the elastic waistband of my drawers tightly I refused to drop them unless my mother turned around. Reluctantly she aimed her broad back at me, obviously afraid of letting me out of her sight for even a moment. The moment my drawers hit the floor I darted up the stairs as naked as Apollo on his way to find Daphne, carrying two thousand years of Oedipus complex into my bedroom.

Digging fresh drawers out of my scarred, painted black bureau—even the furniture was handed down among my race—I thought with surprisingly mature concern that my mother had gone soft in the head. This notion was reinforced when, out my back window, I spotted the lady with the figure of a garbage can clothes-pinning my knotted garments to the laundry line. The sight made me shiver inwardly, and instead of jumping into play clothes I slid under my bed blankets to warm up. There I lay waiting to see what fate had on its schedule for me that cool, late spring morning, a day I should have been studying math instead of a mother who was behaving like a crazy lady on a city street.

Fate stomped up the stairs and lumbered into my room

wearing her ironed-for-church gray dress and matching frown, having now removed her coat. Since I'd always fought being banished to bed, the sight of me under the covers, with the sun still on its way up, caused the cuts in the fig-brown skin under her eyes to deepen. "How you feel, Alexandros?"

At that instant I was the beneficiary of a stroke of sheer brilliance—a flash of racial genius from across the centuries. "Not too hot, mama."

"Too hot?" she moaned, hearing what she wanted to hear. "Where does it burn—in you eyes, you brain, you kidneys? That evil witch!"

Only then did I entirely grasp the source of my mother's madness and, pitifully, I wasted no time in taking advantage of her condition. "I'm feeling kind of . . . achy . . . all over."

"Poor, poor Alex."

As a reward for her sincere worry on my behalf, I closed my eyes as if intending to sleep. But the gesture did more to worry than calm her: Imagine Alex Dropolous Jr. taking a nap before lunch! Through narrow-slitted eyes I watched my mother thump to the window and peer out at my clothes—hanging in knots from the clothesline like great bunches of grapes drying into raisins. Years later I appealed to my mother to reveal the workings of that antidote. For a full minute she stared at the picture of my grandmapou on the bureau, finally stuttering. "It's not good . . . to talk on it, otherwise it won't work next time." From that I gathered she simply didn't know the answer. Like so much in her life, she took Greek matters and myths on unfiltered faith, a commodity so rare in these faithless times we sometimes mistake it for stupidity.

The race home and rapid disrobing must've burned up plenty of energy in me, for a thickness settled into my eyelids that I found impossible to resist. Calmed by a cluster of sparrows cheeping out in the tender grass like kids just released from school, I burrowed into my pillow . . . suddenly dozing off, losing an hour in the caves of my brain. Upon my return I was greeted by a steaming bowl of lemon rice soup. That was not one of my favorites—actually I hated its bitterness, but I'd never had the heart—the guts—to confess this to Evangelina because it would've been like saying "I hate being Greek," because that's what lemon rice soup is all about, being Greek.

Dutifully I sat up and allowed her to puff up the pillows—she had brought a second, a luxury not even my father had been granted in our household, and I responded wearily, exactly the same to all her questions: "Not too hot." Sipping the pungent, foamy fluid tenuously, I was never in any danger of having an appetite inspired in me. All afternoon I managed to sustain this dullness of the senses, and by evening I had won: My mother announced she was keeping me home from school the next day—and rather defensively, too, as if expecting an argument from me.

To deflect possible suspicion I said, though not too enthusiastically, "But mama, I got a big math test tomorrow."

"What's more impotent?" she said, standing firm on what she considered the irreproachable footing of motherhood, "you health or you myth test?"

* * *

When my father slogged into the house around 9 o'clock weighed down by fifteen hours of employees missing in action, shattered dishes, burnt noodle custard at the cafeteria, I heard my mother waylay him at the door. Papou shouted something about "red peppers" to purge himself of the workday—something the anisette he kept stashed in his locker had apparently failed to accomplish that particular day. Then they faded into whispers. Their secrecy made me feel sorry for myself, and I moaned loudly to get Papou to come see me in my remaining hours on earth.

Papou couldn't be fooled as easily as mapou, but he was

perfectly willing to believe if given the chance, so I messed up my hair, held my breath to flush my face, and lowered my eyelids to half mast as he pounded up the stairs. Physically he was a Cambrian boulder, my Papou, with shoulders that would've qualified him to wrestle the Argonauts. He lacked the heroic spirit required for such contests, however, and was loved more for what he didn't do—he was afraid of hurting any living thing, even bugs—than for what he did.

His hair line vanishing like the American wilderness, revealing a forehead creased with concern, he said, "Alex, you don't feel so hot?"

Gravely I rolled my head from side to side. Actually I'd felt just fine until he sat down on the side of the bed and squashed my leg.

"Sorry, Alex," he said, squeezing my calf, but I jerked my leg out of his reach, afraid he might snap the tibia in his massive hands.

In my family it's lemons for whatever ails you, and they will try any trick to get their medicine down your gullet. "If I know'd you was getting sick on me, I woulda brought you slice of lemon meringue pie," he tempted, "on special today." Then he turned his cinder block head toward his wife and said, "Why didn't you call me at work?" knowing perfectly well he would've bitten the receiver in two if he'd been interrupted while trying to feed dozens of Sunday carnivores.

The criticism forced my mother to behave out of character. "Alex didn't eat his lemon soup," she squealed.

My father shook his head gravely. "Lemons—they fix you up fast."

"I know."

"What did this bad lady say to you in Charley's?"

"Nothing, Papou, honest."

Apparently Papou believed more in The Evil Tongue than The Evil Eye, because when he found out she hadn't spoken to me, his forehead smoothed out—even though he must've known Mrs. Rhinosos hadn't spoken to anyone in years. Or maybe he was just in a hurry to get to his red peppers, a taste he had developed, I think, from being around too much boiled food at the cafeteria. Poor Papou: No one had broken the news that we had fled Charley's pepperless. With the chlorine sharpness of Ajax on his hands and the licorice sweetness of anisette on his breath, he tucked me in and, with a pat on my head, assigned me to sleep.

By Monday morning my condition had not improved—and wasn't likely to—not until my classmates had finished tying their brains into knots during the test. An All-American breakfast was one of the few New World extravagances Evangelina permitted in her household, having been won over by the pictures of bright-eyed, smiling kids on Wheaties boxes. But I could manage to swallow only half of the Wheaties, scrambled eggs, sliced oranges, toast with butter and grape jelly, milk, and the wedge of leftover spinach pie that had been slipped in to be on the safe, Greek side.

Though I was sensitive enough to recognize the guilt I owed to family, classmates, teacher and society for lying about my illness, the massive breakfast, the bedside service, the escape from fractions and equations was much too satisfying for me to feel contrite. Not only that, I also felt much too sluggish to repent. At least I was considerate enough to hoist each triangle of toast up to my mouth very slowly, offering her what I believed was a convincing show of infirmity: Nothing's so cruel as a son who deprives his mother of the joys of suffering on his behalf.

Instead of becoming more awake, however, the higher the sun rose the more ill I felt. My throat went dry like an upstate stream in mid-August, my face felt flushed, and I began to ache in places I couldn't reach through my skin—deep, dark, remote territories that were like countries unto themselves, places that seemed more closely related to the soul than to the body. It was as if, as my Aunt Delphinia believes, I had brought on these afflictions by faking them for selfish ends.

None of these symptoms escaped the all-witnessing eyes, ears and nose of Evangelina. Unfortunately, she had to do all the worrying herself, for my father had roller-coasted to work on the Flushing IRT at 5:30 A.M. Every ten minutes or so she clambered into my room and infuriated my bastion of privacy by sticking something into me, somewhere: a nozzle up my nose, cotton swabs into my ears, a tongue depressor down my throat, a thermometer in my rear end—though not without a loud, if ineffectual protest from yours truly.

Since none of these inserts seemed to increase my chances of survival, my mother began to look as if *she* were ill. Her face, normally the color of dry oak leaves, faded to a powdery pallor with her neck exuding a thin coating of greenish grease—no doubt a physical by-product of worry. Then a burning idea got into her head—I knew because her eyes seemed to catch on fire, and she hurried out of the room declaring, "I gotta make phone call."

This announcement alarmed me. I figured she was going to bring Doc Boutrides into the caper. Believing a medical man could take one look at me and know I'd been faking, I said, "Don't spend money on a doctor, Momma. I'm feeling better already."

"No doctor can help with what you got," she warned. "I'm calling Ya-Ya."

I would've been much better off with the doctor.

The family spark plug being called into the case punched a small hole of doubt in my wall of comfort, a wound that was further complicated by a sudden, thickening congestion in my chest. I wasn't sure if I was coming down with a cold; if I was being punished by God for lying; or if the devil actually had been inserted into my soul through the eyes of Mrs. Anna Rhinosos.

* * *

Half an hour after my mother had hung up, into the faded green house of the missing shingles, leaky plumbing, and withered wiring—all upheld by reasonably stable beams—marched my grandmapou Hestiakos, or Ya-Ya Hysterical, as we called her when her hearing aid was turned down. No mourning bread baker draped in black was she, having driven a taxi for years to make ends come reasonably close together. Bouncing around in the front seat of her yellow cab, which always seemed to be dragging a muffler that sent sparks flying, Ya-Ya had learned to bite first and bark later, tell people precisely what she thought of them, and dress without consideration of consequences to herself or her family—such as the time she showed up at the Greek Independence Day Parade, on Fifth Avenue, in a bikini bathing suit due to an unseasonably early hot spell . . . touching off a minor riot: Past seventy years of age, her legs and arms bony as sticks, and with a pair of dried up figs for breasts, she'd still been proud of her flesh.

The story of Ya-Ya swinging a purse loaded with rolls of pennies at a passenger attempting to rob her had made the *Daily News*, and the incident was particularly memorable since she was packaged in such a meager frame—not five foot tall, under one hundred pounds. At the time she still dyed her hair jet black, rubbed obscene rouge into her cheeks, and marked her lips with smears of Passion Flower Red. This presentation—in concert with her cabbie's vocabulary—rattled the gold in the teeth of the Greek patriarchs of the neighborhood, for they went one step further than American men on these points: The woman's place was not merely in the home but at the stove and in the bed.

Compared to Ya-Ya, my mother seemed grave, slow, and gray. Hence the popular assumption that Evangelina was the mother and Hysterical the daughter. More kindly neighbors suggested Evangelina merely had taken after my grandpapou's more conservative side of the family. But that could not be verified since his side of the family had never crossed the Atlantic. Even Papou himself had arrived here late. As the story is told Ya-Ya had somehow gotten hold of a copy of *Police Gazette* as a young married woman in Greece, and though she read no English, the stark black and white photos inspired a passion in her to touch down in the New World. Since Papou refused to have the Greek rushed out of him by American doggedness, Ya-Ya felt compelled to pack her magazine, lipstick, and a fresh change of underwear into a shopping bag and board a steamer for New York. My Aunt Harriet was already a few months in the oven by then.

The young couple corresponded across the Atlantic weekly, monthly. Then nothing. Lonely for male fraternity, I suppose, Ya-Ya drove the cab back to her place one night accompanied by a bald-headed, rough-necked dock-worker from Sardinia. But nothing personal ever passed between them, or so the family liked to believe. Besides, two weeks after they'd met he fled the country to escape immigration authorities—or Ya-Ya, according to her enemies, never to reappear. Which was just as well since Ya-Ya Hysterical's spouse, my dear Papou, showed up in Brooklyn the next week carrying a couple of battered suitcases, his mouth filled with apologies, his hand clutching a cluster of dried up daisies.

* * *

With rowdy vigor the diminutive trooper stormed into my room wearing—so help me—pink shorts and a black leather jacket. Ya-Ya began interrogating me, while my mother wavered darkly behind her in that fat gray dress, looking like an assistant torturer rather than a loving mother. All that was missing was the whip.

"How long did Mrs. Rhinosos stare at you?" Ya-Ya shrieked.

"I don't know!" I wailed.

"Did she smile at you?"

"I don't remember!" I wailed, and I really didn't remember.

"Did you look in her eyes?"

"I don't think so!" I wailed.

"Evangelina, get me steel wool–I gonna scrub Alex's tongue for lying."

Suddenly it all came back to me. I mean, I decided to invent answers to her questions to keep her from doing something crazy. "Mrs. Rhinosos stared straight through me," I claimed, "right into my bones!"

The mothers glanced at each other with blunt, racial significance, and then Ya-Ya began behaving as if she were Hippocrates on a mission of healing: She took my pulse; felt my forehead with the back of her hand; put her ear against my chest; jabbed my rib cage with her pointy nails; next she scrutinized my toe nails, apparently to see if they had blackened; looked intimately at the roots of my hair as if searching for lice; and asked my mother about the mole on my neck: "How long has he had this?" she insinuated.

In one united huff they quit my room: Down in the living room their voices dropped drastically, shutting me out of their conversation. The next sounds I heard were the rapidly opening and shutting of cabinets in the kitchen, plus other noises I couldn't figure out–though I tried my damnedest, slipping out of bed to aim my ear out the door.

"Get under those covers, *Vreh*!" my grandmother roared, uncorking one of her uncanny powers–to know what another is doing without seeing him do it.

Leaping into bed, I squeaked, "I *am* under the covers!" In ten minutes they returned to my room looking like a pair of paramedics moving toward me with grim animation, the way they had moved down the aisle at Mary's funeral. While I had no desire to wade into deep water during a lightning storm like my cousin, I suspected a similar shock treatment was in store for me. At the same time I understood I was powerless against them—though Greek men dominate their women, the women get back at them by dominating the male children.

Once they had me surrounded, a small jar of fluid materialized in Ya-Ya's hand the way a magician will amaze witnesses by making something appear in his empty hand. A black cross was crayoned on the cap, a symbol that raised a terrified awe in me, along with the fuzzy hairs on the back of my neck. The substance was the color of urine that had been left around a long while—deep gold, and with a flash of horror I realized they were going to make me drink it.

"No!" I wailed. "Noooooooo!"

My mother responded by grabbing my shoulders roughly, as if I were a patient in a loony bin. Before that grappling of my person I had never appreciated the strength in those flabby arms: like most boys of ten, I believed I already had developed bigger muscles than my mother, if not my father.

Apparently age has some rights in these rites, for it was my grandmapou who unscrewed the cap and dipped two fingers adorned with long plastic nails into the jar. Before I could so much as blink the old dame had clutched my jaw with her other claw and made a slick crucifix on my forehead with her wet fingers. Gratified I hadn't been forced to drink the stuff, I didn't struggle when she did the same to my shoulders, each of my hands, feet and, inevitably, to my heart. Among my kind, everything ultimately winds up at the heart.

Unexpectedly I became quite calm—possibly because I'd caught a whiff of harmless olive oil with some sort of spice stirred in. The mothers backed off and looked me over, putting their heads together as if conferring on an especially complicated case. While they deliberated I began to realize it would be to my advantage to allow their prescription to cure me. That way I could begin preparing them to deal with the notion that I would be going back to school the next day.

If only plans would work out as planned: An hour after Ya-Ya had greased my forehead, my mother brought lunch—Campbell's Cream of Celery, plus a glass of milk and a block of feta cheese. But I didn't have the spirit to eat, an early symptom of my worsening condition: I barely touched the food on the tray. Luckily Ya-Ya and my mother had gone downstairs, otherwise they would've made a scene over my lack of appetite. As the afternoon waned, so did I, and though the late sun dealt ribs of yellow warmth across my bed, I felt chilly in my innards. And the weaker I grew, the more difficult it became to fight off the idea that I had indeed been afflicted by The Evil Eye.

As my eyes grew narrower, the eyes of my Greek guardians grew wider, and by early evening it became obvious to them that neither the knotted trousers nor the oily crosses had generated sufficient spiritual influence to deflect Mrs. Rhinosos' powerful gaze; instinctively they understood that something drastic had to be done if my body and soul were to be salvaged. None of this was stated to me, yet it was all only too apparent in their fear-crimped faces, as the sun softened at the edges and the evening began to sketch itself in charcoal into the sky.

Before they could tackle this crisis, even before Papou had gotten home from work, I had escaped into sleep . . . a hectic, tossing-and-turning sleep. Most of the night I spent running breathlessly up and down the broken marble steps of the Temple of Zeus, followed closely, greasily, vastly by Mrs. Rhinosos, who had grown long green talons, and who somehow managed to keep pace with me even though she never seemed to run—apparently bounced along after me like a huge human balloon tied to my neck.

* * *

When I awoke Tuesday, tired from all that running, Papou had already gone to work. I missed him. He didn't take The Evil

Eye as seriously as the women. Though I felt somewhat better, the well-being didn't last since I immediately had a visitation from the mothers . . . probably they'd been lurking outside my door, waiting for my eyes to blink open. It was so early I wondered if Ya-Ya had stayed the night. If so, she had not been sitting around biting her nails, for she swept her arm toward the door like an M.C. on a stage, and into my very own room marched Father Nick, as if he were the featured artist in a variety show.

Dressed in floor-length black robes and a funny little round cap that made him look Jewish, Father Nick was of middling height, but was as dark and handsome as I imagine the devil must be: He had a curly black moustache, extended side burns lightly brushed with silver, a classic chiseled chin, and silvery gray eyes that seemed intimately acquainted with one's innermost secrets. Especially women's secrets. Whenever he appeared, the parish women would wiggle with what I prefer to think was an offering of spiritual joy. But there were no wiggles just then, only gravity in my grandmother and her daughter, and from the look on his face it was clear Father Nick considered himself to be on a mission of mercy.

"And good morning, Alex."

"'Morning, Father Nick."

"And how are we doing?" he said, slipping me a bit of that elementary psychology of sharing in my misfortune without, of course, actually sharing in it.

"Okay."

"And is your scalp itchy this morning?"

"No, Father."

"And are the kidneys troubled?"

"I don't think so, Father."

"That's a good boy, Alex."

Just when I figured there was nothing to worry about, I saw it: a tube of clear, no doubt blessed water in his strong, manicured fingers. "I want you to drink these," he said, as if there were several.

Already I was beginning to learn not to struggle against the inevitable, so I separated my jaws as Father Nick popped the cork and brought the tiny bottle to my lips. But it was only when he was spilling the tepid fluid onto my tongue that I noticed there was something weird—a hairy white root, or maybe the fetus of a rat—floating at the bottom of the bottle. I coughed harshly, trying to expel the stuff, but it was too late: Down my throat the fluid rolled like beads of mercury, causing me to cough again and shake like I was having a bout of hypothermia.

"Good to the last drop," he smiled, quoting a coffee commercial to prove how modern, how Americanized he was.

Courageously I managed to grant him the obliged response: "Thank . . . you . . . Father."

"And don't spit rest of the day, Alex," was the last thing he said to me, turning with the grace of David Niven and gliding out of my room, followed too closely by his devoted parishioners.

The wicked trio had a pow-wow down in the vestibule, Father Nick's deep, mellow voice rising through the house, theirs more like high-pitched chirrups. Ya-Ya and my mother thanked him again and again, and I heard him say, "Oh, I almost forgot—this is for Alex." Their sighs of appreciation were audible all the way upstairs. Now what? I wondered. Finally they saw him out the door, and in three minutes they were back in my room. Heading toward me with an obtrusive single-mindedness, Ya-Ya flipped open the lid of a small blue box. Instinctively I lurched away, expecting a black spider to jump out. But the box contained nothing more than a tiny pin—a porcelain eye, with a blue center and white and gray rings around it, set on a brass clasp.

"When I pin this *filakto* on you pajamas," she instructed,

"don't take it off for no reason—you hear me?" Consistent with her style of stark realism, she made a chopping gesture with her hand. "Or I break you neck!"

I nodded gravely as she decorated me, presumably for bravery beyond the call.

"Don't play with it," my mother warned, "or you wear off the blessing."

With the regularity of nurses on pill duty, every half hour one or the other came up to check me over—the stairs having grown steeper to their aging knees over the two days. Again they inspected my toe nails, the roots of my hair, looked up my nose and in my ears. Past noon they appeared together, armed with lunch, their jaws extended as if daring me to try to get out of eating. For the first time since the previous morning I felt hungry, or who knows to what lengths they may have gone to torture me: I gobbled down an egg salad sandwich and finished a mug lemon rice soup in self defense, plus two glasses of milk. But the women had lived through too many spells to be swayed by one satisfactory lunch.

Partly because I was very hungry, and partly to escape that mad house, that evening I swallowed everything they loaded onto my tray, as if I were a starving goat in the foothills of Mount Kajmakcalan: three chopped up potatoes, two lamb chops, two helpings of spinach (which I despise), three pieces of buttered homemade bread, a side order of lima beans, two glasses of iced tea with slices of lemons. But it was when I wiped out the last of four anise seed cookies that my grandmother agreed to leave me in my mother's custody. Ya-Ya's departure was marked by her taking credit for my recovery: "I knew it," she said to Evangelina. "Always make the cross of olive oil with oregano and lemon sauce!"

* * *

After three days in the grips of two Greek mothers, I was anxious to get back among my own kind. The idea of school no longer seemed so terrible, with or without a make-up exam. Though my mother went a round or two with me the next morning, I finally convinced her—mostly by forcing down two bowls of Wheaties—I was feeling perfectly well enough to go back to school; that my system had been purged of the ill effects of The Evil Eye. With heavy gusts of exhalation she released me unto the world.

"If you see Mrs. Rhinosos, you run back home. You hear?"

"Yes, Momma, I hear."

For the first time in three days I entered the great outdoors of New York City, my mother looking harried, rushed-into old-age as she waved weakly at the door. With effervescent sunlight splashing onto the sidewalks, and my life stretching out before me like the blue porcelain skies of that spring day, the two-story shoe box houses seemed wondrous edifices from which to set out into the world . . . the green and red and blue and white doors lined up along the streets like the colorful beliefs that make our lives worth living.

Happy Thesmophoria!

As everyone wandering from sea to shining sea knows, Thanksgiving is an emblematic American holiday devoted to feasting gratefully and lavishly throughout the land of pumpkin pie. Despite this undeniable truth, my family of Greek patriots—some born in this country, some not, set aside their Old Country customs every November to salute, and tear into, the fat-breasted, roasted turkey. So vigorously do they observe Thanksgiving that many witnesses to this annual ceremony believe descendants of these transplanted Hellenics stood centuries ago among those black-pantaloon-wearing pilgrims, extending their hands to deer skin-wrapped native Americans; that they had sat down at a log-hewn table to share an abundant feast with these peaceable tribesmen; that present-day Greek revelers have gone so far as to claim sovereignty over this red, white, and blue celebration, as if it were yet another of the gifts of enlightenment—along with philosophy, sculpture, and science—that they'd bestowed on western civilization.

* * *

At one such holiday jamboree, not many years ago, sundry Aegean-loyalists had begun trickling from different neighborhoods of New York City into our family's Brooklyn headquarters—a fire-escape embraced, three-story, half-refurbished, old ladies home. Their procession started just past noon, and though the turkey was still being basted every half hour in the oven, family and friends began milling around our majestically long table—sectioned together from two eight-foot long by four-foot wide sheets of plywood aligned over police barriers. (These wooden "horses" had been appropriated late one night, the previous week, from a construction site on Flatbush Avenue.) Because the planks were so immense, the table meant to bring family closer together actually had the opposite effect—attendees had to waggle their hands wildly to be seen and squawk loudly to be heard. To spruce up this crude dining apparatus, three paper table cloths—imprinted with autumn-tinted leaves, acorns, and pumpkins—were tacked onto its splintery surface.

At the head of this grand, make-shift table, as if ruling from his throne atop Mount Olympus, sat my Papou, properly jazzed up with an orange-and-black checkered bowtie clipped at the Adam's apple atop his striped blue shirt. Hovering over the rickety chair at the distant end of this wooden plateau was my Uncle Stavros, also dressed in his finest—neck strangled by a red-and-yellow spotted tie tucked into the folds of his ragged gaberdine suit jacket. Around both sides of this vast serving surface swirled the following family members and associates: Christos, Cousin Pavlos, Delphinia, Euthalia Damocles, Mrs. Crousious, Uncle Kosmas, Cousin Peter, Cousin Mary, Aunt Harriet, and me, Alexandros Jr. A piano bench near the doorway supported the double-wide rear end of our neighborhood witch, Mrs. Rhinosos. Not yet stationed in this de facto police line up were Evangelina and Ya-Ya, both of whom were on kitchen duty.

Already the early arrivals had begun plucking spanakopita, celery stalks, black olives, chunks of feta, and carrot sticks off the oval platters planted in the middle. Meanwhile Evangelina kept zipping out of the kitchen and into the dining area to check on whether every place at the table was equipped with the appropriate dining tools. During each visit she also warned us to "stop chewing up all the appetizers," insisting *every* family member had to be in attendance before anyone could be permitted to pop an olive into his or her jaws. (Still missing from the list of invited guests were Merrula Tarsipias, her youngest son Harry, and her older son Henry.)

"On Thanksgiving everyone in family must join hands at the table and eat together," said Evangelina, not bothering to explain how we could eat and hold hands at the same time.

As we sat squirming on our metal, wooden, and plastic mostly folding chairs—many of them borrowed from neighbors, waiting for the late comers to show up, all of us were gradually embraced by the penetrating aromas of the chubby, butter-brushed turkey roasting merrily in the oven; the honey-dipped slices of apples; the bubbling peppered corn pudding; the sputtering creamed squash casserole; the yogurt-lemon muffins doubling in size in that same dark cavern.

At twenty past one o'clock two more of our contingent—looking rushed and flustered and apologetic—materialized at our table: Aunt Merrula and her son Harry. "Sorry we so late," she said with a gush of Greecian guilt. "Had to clean apartment for holiday—filthy!" In a half whisper she added: "Henry can't make it today."

In a reasonable facsimilie of a Greek chorus several members of my family piped in unison, "Henry won't be celebrating Thanksgiving with his family?"

"He had to go to his office for business meeting."

"Since when does Henry have an office?" Stavros inquired, raising his bushy eyebrows a full inch.

"Oh yes," Merrula exclaimed. "Henry's a working boy now."

"What kinda work?" Papou said, though I believe he already had a good idea.

"Sales."

"Selling what?" Stavros intervened, though I believe he already could answer his own question.

"Small business insurance."

Papou and Uncle Stavros glanced at each other from the remote, opposite ends of the table, locking their eyes on each other a moment before raising them toward the ceiling as if searching for wayward angels.

Ya-Ya hobbled into the area. "Henry not coming?"

"No, he has a business meeting," I explained.

Ya-Ya spat: "How can he have business meeting?—everything's locked today."

Peter yelped: "Even the post office is closed."

Ruefully, Mary wondered out loud: "Would it be right for the family to enjoy Thanksgiving dinner without my brother Henry at the table?"

"God will forgive us," Stavros assured her, revealing just how intent he was on slicing into the turkey's rib cage: He liked to do all the carving.

Christos agreed: "It would be a mortal sin to let that beautiful bird go to waste."

"Along with its drumsticks," I added, unable to stop myself from putting in a claim for at least one of the turkey's meaty thighs.

Though no one had asked, Papou said moodily, "If you ask me, lately Henry's too much the big shot to eat a meal with family."

"How can you say such a thing?" Merrula snapped back at him.

"Henry just takes his job to heart."

Under her breath Ya-Ya murmured, "To heart? Took him forever to go to work."

"Since it's Thanksgiving," Uncle Kosmas suggested, "why don't we all forgive Henry and just go ahead and fill our bellies."

"Forgive him—why?" Papou piped up. "Once again Henry only thinks of himself—cares nothing about family."

Merrula protested: "Henry brings money into our family kitchen."

To put this squabble behind him, I suppose, Papou took a

long pull on his goblet of wine: a thick, murky red, too sweet, syrupy substance, the fourth glass he'd consumed in twenty minutes—I'd counted every one of them. Later, during dinner, he also emptied a shot glass of anisette and two of metaxa. It was the first time I'd paid attention to my father's close friendship with alcohol. Who knows?—maybe this had been going on a lot longer than I'd realized. My loving, caring Papou—a drinking man? It didn't sound right. Sure I'd heard him slur a few words at a wedding party, but this felt different—more like an earnest commitment.

* * *

With nods of the head and waves of the hand it was established that we would uncork the Greek version of this American holiday without Henry in attendance. And why not? Many of us had skipped breakfast so we would have room in our tummies for the turkey, the fixings, the desserts, and the wine.

The procession of women began, led by Ya-Ya and followed dutifully by aunts Delphinia and Merrula. Even Aunt Harriet, the family outcast, had deigned to serve. All were dressed in "house dresses"—loosely fitting, flower-printed, non-descript wrappings that made all of them appear much older than they were. Each upheld a platter or dish or bowl filled to the brim with fruits of the season—cobs of corn with their shiny buttered kernels, a mountain of mashed sweet potatoes with maple syrup drippings in the center, mounds of olive-oiled vegetables—acorn squash, brown-sugared carrots, cauliflower, string beans, peas mixed with tiny white onions, broccoli sprinkled with crumbs of goat cheese. In straggled Cousin Mary clinging to a cracked, massive bowl of stuffing—chestnuts, white rice, sweet sausages, chopped celery and onions mishmashed together. At last, Evangelina wobbled grandly into the dining space balancing the crispy-skinned, forlorn-looking, twenty-eight pound star of the show—the fresh-killed turkey sprawled out on a huge clay platter.

Before too many minutes had wafted away into the bright sunlight on that chilly autumn day, everyone had managed to claim their preassigned chairs. Only Henry's chair remained empty. Instantly the serving spoons, clamps, and prongs began to flash and clink over the table as wads of still-steaming foods were scooped out of their splattered nests—and plopped like dung onto two sets of supermarket coupon dishes: Each bore the sketch of a New England hamlet, the kind of steeple-dominated crossroad where the first Thanksgiving might have convened.

In between cheerful chatter and rowdy exclamations and ill-timed jokes, we attacked these soft volcanoes of human fodder, often swallowing forkfuls before we'd had a chance to chew them down to size: everything looked so authentically Thanksgiving, and tasted so acutely delicious! All so satisfying that, as we gorged our gullets determinedly, the family stopped yelping and laughing and whistling and, instead, emitted a low, group humming. And during a pause in the protracted process of filling my gut, I idly scanned the length and breadth of our jam-packed table—studying the gaggle of Greek braggarts that is my family. At that moment, quite unexpectedly, something way down in my psyche caused me to blurt these words loudly: "This is just like Thesmophoria!"

Several pairs of eyes zeroed in on me, each asking bluntly: What the hell is *Thesmophoria*? Honestly, I was just as puzzled as they were, but while they continued to question me with their eyes, tidbits of info related to that peculiar word popped into my head: Two thousand years ago, the married women of Athens celebrated a festival they called *Thesmophoria* to honor Demeter, goddess of harvest. Hades, god of the underworld, had kidnapped Demeter's young daughter, Persephone, and having grown deeply depressed over this loss, Demeter was unwilling to feed the population unless she could be reunited with her daughter. By late autumn, a compromise had been reached between Hades and Demeter, and so the goddess allowed the harvest to proceed so the world could be fed. That's when Thesmophoria was established to honor Demeter and Persephone. I was stunned—where had I acquired this stuff? I didn't even know I'd picked up and stored this knowledge somewhere in the depths of my brain. Or, who knows, maybe it had simply risen on its own out of the deepest corners in my Greek soul.

Well, I certainly wasn't the only one who was stunned—many of my Greek compatriots had twisted their necks in my direction, and were demanding an explanation, so I was forced to present the bits and pieces of that ancient mythology which had come to me. While I was doing this, I also kept trying to figure out where and how I'd come across such knowledge. Had I read about *Thesmophoria* in one of my class text books? Had I witnessed this festival acted out in a movie or on television? Or was this knowledge merely a form of racial memory, bequeathed to me by reason of my birth as a Greek?

"These intelligent Greek women would celebrate *Thesmophoria* for three days," I expounded. "Eating, drinking, making merry. Very much like Thanksgiving is celebrated for one day in America."

Uncle Stavros was the first to react to what I'd said. "Isn't that just a myth? These festivals didn't really happen, did they?"

His question took me by surprise, so I had to choose the words of my response carefully: "Stories are made up from what people feel, what they do, and what they believe," my tone suggesting I knew what I was talking about. "Even when these stories are myths, they can have a powerful impact on people—which means they might as well have happened."

This idea I'd fabricated out of that vivid autumn air seemed to float beyond Stavros's comfort zone, so he hoisted the gravy bowl and dumped a thick, lumpy brown coating over the slab of white meat on his plate; it almost seemed as if he were using the gravy not to add flavor to his turkey but to shield himself from something he didn't quite grasp.

* * *

Some time past three o'clock, after the family had launched a frontal attack on the dessert platters—baklava, revani cake, melopita sifnos, galaktoboureko, plus pumpkin pie to be on the traditional side, Father Nick appeared at our door resembling a ghost of himself: the pallid face, neck, and hands presented a stark contrast to his totally black attire. Despite his bloodless appearance, he appeared to be his usual, strong bodied self. His broad shoulders were squared off like a boxer's; the muscles in his neck looked like steel pipes; his fingers were sinewy with power: It was as if he'd been able to build up his bodily strength by wrestling with the devil for many years.

"I am visiting families of the St. Demetrius congregation for Thanksgiving," and when he said this, I suddenly understood why he'd been putting on more weight lately. Just how many feasts, I wondered, should one man of God undergo?

"Please come in Father Nick," several of us chirped.

Once the family had made a place for Father Nick at our table—he took over Henry's unoccupied chair, the holy man cast his pearly gray eyes over each and every one of us. Seeming to look straight through skin and bones directly into our souls, he declared, "Happy Thesmophoria to one and all!"

Thesmophoria! Every face at the table immediately took on that queer look of curiosity again, and for a moment or two I lost my breath: I was stupendously surprised that some one other than myself had knowledge of that strange word. But upon further reflection, it made sense that the possessor of such knowledge would be Father Nick. Before he'd arrived on the shores of America, he'd completed an intense orthodox education in Athens, and he'd always struck me as acutely curious about everything he came in contact with. Especially when it involved Greek history.

"Let us begin with a prayer of Thanksgiving, *okie-dokie*?" Father Nick liked to use American expressions to prove he had adapted well to his new circumstances.

Father Nick, the tallest and sturdiest among us, stood straight and steady in his pressed black suit and stretched his arms wide over the table so as to include everyone in the room. "Father in heaven, we have come together in your holy shadow to thank you for the countless blessings you have granted to every one of us over many years. Please allow us to remain close to you and to each other on this holiday of thankfulness. Amen."

Earnestly the congregants echoed "Amen," and a moment later the gaggle burst into a subdued jubilation, as if we'd all just been freed to return home after a very long day of harvesting corn in the fields. The forks, knives, and spoons went sweeping over the dessert platters. Except for my own utensils. I was still too shocked by, and curious about, his use of that singular word, and because I was seated almost directly across from the good man, I felt emboldened to say: "Father Nick, if you please, could you tell me how a man of God such as yourself happens to know about the pagan festival called Thesmophoria?"

"Ah yes, Thesmophoria," he articulated, pausing a moment as if remembering the exact moment he'd first come across that word. "When I was a boy in Athens, my mother told me all about this festival."

"Your mother?"

"Oh yes, Greek mythology fascinated my beloved mother—may God rest her soul in heaven."

"Please, Father Nick, would you mind telling me what she told you about Thesmophoria?"

While the others at the table were inserting slices of pie

and hunks of cake into their mouths, he said in a rather high-pitched voice: "At first there was a day of fasting at Thesmophoria. On the following two days mountains of food and seas of wine were served! Celebrants listened to the playing of flutes and lyres. Many danced bare-footed at the Olympian Temple of Zeus. Especially popular were the competitions—in one they raced in and out of the marble columns of the Acropolis. Winners were awarded prizes."

"Really? What sorts of prizes?"

"Baby pigs, lambs, goats, and these animals were then slaughtered and roasted in a communal fire."

"Father Nick, *Thesmophoria* sounds like it must've been quite a wild pagan event."

"More than anything, Alex, it was a religious celebration of fertility."

Amidst the din of Greeks gabbing about the high prices of lamb and devouring sweet delicacies, my noble priest kept going on about this ancient festival. "In Greece at the time, women were excluded from many activities. With Thesmophoria, it was the men who were excluded." All the while I couldn't stop questioning in my mind how this man of God had become so interested in this pagan rite. But when he told me that these women "took a boy off the streets of Athens to be offered up to Tartarus, god of the deep abyss," I asked him: "Father Nick, what do you mean by 'offered up'?"

"The boy was led to the top of the Methana Volcano and sacrificed to thank the gods for giving them Thesmophoria."

"Sacrificed—you don't mean killed, do you?"

"The boy was tied to a post, wrapped in branches gathered from lemon trees, and the pyre was set on fire."

Impossible! How could the civilized wives of the great philosophers and artists and scientists of ancient Greece have sacrificed young boys as an act of thanksgiving? Father Nick must've gotten the details of this festival all wrong. Or his mother had related horribly incorrect information to him. The final possibility to occur to me was that everything he'd told me had been a bundle of lies! Had my spiritual leader, the most holy Father Nicholas, the friend I trusted more than anyone else—lied about all of it?

In a moment Father Nick surprised, confused, then enlightened me by transforming that ghostly stiffness of his face into a wide, almost laughing smile. Instantly I understood that the man dressed in black from his feet to his neck hadn't been lying so much as telling me a colorful, mythological story from ancient Greece; that because Thanksgiving was a joyful day of gratitude for our many blessings, purely for the fun of it my much-respected priest had gifted me with a half hour of lively entertainment. Telling stories, after all, is very different from telling lies.

Silent Night in the
Holy Land of Brooklyn

Just before I'd landed in my teenaged years, toward the bitter end of December, I found myself untangling garland on our lumpy couch in Brooklyn, nursing a case of holiday blues: "It just doesn't feel like Christmas" I said to whatever spirits, past or present, might be cowering in the far corners of our parlor. Yet all the distinctive ingredients of the season were present: the arousing aroma of a tray of buttery *kourabiedes* being slid out of the oven by my mother, a boys' choir trilling "Silent Night" over the buzzing radio, pop of hot coals in the furnace, crushed walnuts and softening apples and striped peppermint candies, all accented by the tinkle of a plastic icicle against a Christmas ball . . . made of a glass no thicker than that membrane in the soul which separates the child from the adult.

After the icy face of day had sunk behind the line-up of two-story residential houses across the street, my father was shouldered into the outer hall from the porch by a blast of cold air. As if trying to fill that hollow sensation in my chest, I looped the last strand of garland onto the fir tree and scampered out to the hallway: I wanted to size up the last-minute bundles he always brought home the evening before the big day. Papou's face looked gray, and his hands were empty.

While peering toward the kitchen my father spoke to me: "How is tree coming 'long?"

"Only the tinsel's left to put on," I piped. "Want to see it?"

Without a word he stalked past me, pushing through the

swinging door into the kitchen. I remained in the shadows between the parlor and kitchen, immobilized by the dark cloud he had left in his wake. Knock, knock, knock, knock sounded the knife against the cutting board: My mother was chopping celery stalks into half-inch U's—to be stirred into soup, diced into salad. While acknowledging his entrance with a murmur, she obviously didn't want to be distracted from the too-many duties before her. Knock, knock, knock, knock.

"Evangelina," my father began. "When I'm leaving coffee shop, my brother-in-law calls me from Chicago. . . ."

"What happened?" she asked, a pinch of alarm in her voice.

"It's Helen. . . ."

The chopping stopped. "Oh no."

My father's throat made a noise, and though I knew better than to be listening to my parents' conversation, I felt unable to move out of hearing range.

"On the eve of the Lord's birth," my mother lamented.

"Poor, poor Helen," moaned my father.

"Poor Helen," my mother repeated.

Silence took hold of the kitchen a few moments before I heard my mother ask, "What do you want to do, Alex?"

My father's voice dragged like a medieval dirge: "She's going to be . . . laid out Christmas day."

"Christmas day? Why Christmas day?"

Only then did I understand what had happened, but knowing didn't make me feel any different. To me Aunt Helen had as much reality as a bright print of Mrs. Claus on a Christmas card. Only a few times over the years, at a wedding or christening or funeral, had she materialized with her husband close by her side. All I remembered about them is that she had red-streaked eyes and coughed a lot, and his arms dangled out of his short-sleeved shirt like a pair of unusually long, splotchy sausages. They were accompanied by three boys who, husky as neighborhood bullies, were unilaterally, irritatingly attached to my life: "Say hello to your cousins!"

When my mother broke the silence again, I realized I'd been staring at the frying-pan-shaped clock which hung on the wall over the telephone table: "With the holidays, it's going to be hard to catch a train or bus." In those days an airplane never occurred to them.

"Maybe I drive the car," my father muttered.

That comment must've widened my mother's eyes. Like the family to which its care had been entrusted, the car had been behaving eccentrically lately: In October and November a mechanic had leaned over its swelled fenders with a puzzled expression, managing only to change its spark plugs and air filter but without the desired results.

"Maybe you should stay home on Christmas day, Alex," said his wife, "and go out on the 26th . . . for services. . . ."

In my mind I could see them standing motionless like cardboard cut-outs in the kitchen, which was cluttered with batter-coated bowls and stained sheets of wax-paper and un-capped jars, staring past one another, each waiting for the other to say something. At last my father agreed, with a minimum of words, that it was probably best to remain within walls he knew, that knew him, for Christmas; and then to make his way to his sister's side "for the last time in this life."

I heard movement. Just in time I scurried into the parlor, climbed up on the bench—somewhat shakily, and resumed tossing silvery strings of tinsel across the upraised, prickly branches. With heavy footsteps my father entered and came right up to my bench, the height of which enabled me to look at him without having to tilt my head too far back. Gazing at the white, fragile glass star on the highest stem, he said: "Alex, your Aunt Helen in Chicago"—he made that noise again.

"I know, Papa," I confessed, saving me from having to hear the words spoken face to face. He stood there with his lips drawn into his face, looking at me as if there was something

I was supposed to say. But I didn't know what it was. With nothing to hold onto up on my perch, I became slightly dizzy and, fearing I might fall, stepped down off the bench to where he could see the top of my head again.

He turned away, lumbered to the phone table in the hallway, and began dialing. Once, twice. On his third try he got through to Chicago. The conversation was brief, and I heard him conclude: "On Christmas I eat with my family. Next day I sit with my sister." After replacing the receiver in its cradle, he stood stiff and still in the weak glow of a bulb with a trembling filament, as if he too had stopped breathing.

Later, just as I had finished glazing the tree with tinsel, Alexandros Sr. carried a jigger of anisette to his big, bulky armchair near the window, sat down, and began sipping the licorice-flavored liquor. Seeing such a large man drinking from such a little glass struck me as comical: He was at least six feet tall, weighed over two hundred pounds, had a neck as thick as a telephone pole, and eyebrows as tough as the brush on a street-cleaner's broom. Yet for all his physical marvels he was usually so unobtrusive, so respectful, so quiet, I sus-pect he took up very little space in people's minds. Helen, two years older, had been his only sister, and his younger, only brother Constantine had undergone a "routine procedure" in Cleveland years earlier which had routinely sent him to his grave. His mother and father, too, had been freed from their cares. Half buried in an armchair too soft to uphold so broad and heavy a mass, he looked truly alone in the world.

* * *

Christmas morning came anyway, and I found my green felt stocking hung from the doorknob of my bedroom closet, stuffed like a five-pound bag of potatoes, yet looking some-what forlorn, as if it were the last banner of childhood. In the pearly light of post-dawn I fingered the dimpled tangerines and icy marbles and almonds sealed in waffled shells. Round and oblong candies were stuck to the felt, making them furry but nonetheless edible. And out of its toe I dug the leftover change from my father's pockets.

Down the stairs I bounded in my thin cotton pajamas, chilly in the morning air. In the moment it took to dash from the archway into the parlor, the shimmering garland, the sting of pine resin, the striped sheen of candy canes, the presents topped with red and green bows—all of it had finally added up to Christmas. Upstairs I could hear my parents stirring out of bed, but I had not yet been equipped with sufficient patience to wait for them. Under the outstretched branches I crawled, the jellybeans of colored lights hot near my face, my arms deep in packages, in mysteries—concealed in crinkly paper imprinted with jaunty reindeer and grinning couples in horse-drawn sleighs and country villages blanketed by snow. With a rising joy I searched for my name on gift tags and tore away one secret after another: new ice skates, new basketball, new erector set, and the inevitable socks, which struck me as old rather than new.

Thumping down the stairs they came. He wore shiny black trousers and a faded white shirt, both recently pressed. She wore a brown house dress with pockets the color and shape of snowballs. "Couldn't you wait for momma and papa?" my mother asked of me, smiling to herself as she made her way into the kitchen. My father simply nodded at no one in particular and sank into his armchair.

"Look what I got for Christmas," I said, as if he didn't know, extending the erector set toward him with both hands, wanting him to test its weight and, thereby, its importance. But he kept his hands to himself, staring at the chest solemnly, as if it were a miniature coffin made out of tin.

In a few minutes my mapou entered the parlor carrying two great mugs of steaming coffee, and seeing me cross-legged on the rug, locking pieces of the erector set together, she said, "Maybe you can build me bigger kitchen, Alex."

Once they'd finished nursing their coffees, my parents began opening their gifts, though much more slowly than I had done: for my mother, a heavy wooden salad bowl with a giant spoon and fork, a housecoat, stockings and, from me, Evening in Paris toilet water; for my father, a tool kit, two pairs of huge underpants, striped suspenders and, from me, imitation leather slippers. While my mother tried on the satiny pink house coat and turned around to show it off, my father stared at the wrenches as if he no longer understood what use tools could be to anyone.

It was not until well after we had picked at the roasted leg of lamb and mashed potatoes and boiled spinach and biscuits that the excitement over my gifts wafted away, my spirits sinking as low as the mercury in the thermometer: Once again, it just didn't feel like Christmas. That was also around the time I found myself thinking about what my father might be feeling, with his sister stretched out dead in Chicago. But I thought about this only briefly, only shallowly: I didn't understand my father any more than I did death.

* * *

By late afternoon, looking out the front window, I noticed metallic shavings of snow had begun twirling out of the sky, settling like cake frosting on the sidewalks, garbage cans, and the hood of our car. As darkness rushed forward the patches of whiteness widened, stacking up against lamp posts and fences and porch stairs. The wind seemed to be gushing up out of the sewer gratings, attempting to fling the snow back where it came from. Occasionally a frigid fury shook the loose house, and I imagined trucks stalled out on the snow-thickening parkway, and tugboats in the harbor being thrashed by wind-driven crystals.

The cold having edged deeper and deeper into the house, my father hoisted his body up and tramped out into the hallway, down the groaning wooden stairs, onto the chilled, uneven basement floor that was peppered with black dust. We heard the shovel scrape into the bin, lumps of coal clatter against the iron innards of the furnace. Up the stairs he marched, scuffing down the hallway into the parlor, and going straight to the window. Holding the leaden drape aside, he said to himself: "How will I find Helen in this snow?"

Glancing toward me, Evangelina raised the cumbersome load of her body off the sofa and said to her husband: "I go pack some things so we can start early in the morning." Through the parlor, toward the stairway in the hall she moved. In a moment she had disappeared. The house creaked in the wind, and I noticed someone had turned off the holiday music on the radio.

Just then it came to me that I too would be disconnected from my home—transported halfway across the country on the day after Christmas, the second best day of the year—the day we become better acquainted with our gifts; what I didn't understand at the time is that I would also be forced to relinquish the most precious gift of the season—a suspension in growing up, and with the prospect of having to face the ultimate fact of life.

Usually a few visitors would drop by on Christmas day, but the snow and wind kept even the lonely close to their radiators that year. Instead of carrying packages through wind and snow, relatives and neighbors telephoned—Aunt Delphinia and Uncle Stavros and Birdie O'Brien and Aunt Merrula—wishing us a happy holiday, asking what gifts we'd found under our tree. Not even the cheerful ring of the phone succeeded in melting the frozen gloom. Especially since my father had to repeat several times into the receiver, in that low rumble, that his sister Helen's lungs had given up on her, and she now lay cold and quiet before rows of folding chairs in Chicago . . . when she should have been home unwrapping gifts with her family.

The storm and my father seemed to be in conspiracy, taking the polish out of the new copper tea kettle, the joy out of the toys under the tree, and I experienced a grown-up desire to breathe happiness into his heart, the way the furnace puffed hot air into the cold rooms. But I didn't know how to go about undertaking such an enormous task. Instead I sat there pressing ridges into my fingers against the bright nickel blades of the skates.

My father edged like a snow drift over to the tree, close to where I sat on that braided scatter rug, a little island of scrap cloth. While standing, he tried to force his feet into the slippers I'd gotten him—too small. Always I got him slippers, gloves that were too small, a result, I suppose, of my too looking upon him as smaller than he really was.

"Thank you for slippers," he said to me for the second time, which was just about all he said to me that day.

"Sorry they don't fit so good, Papou."

"They fit."

My father drifted back to his armchair and dropped down onto the hollowed-out cushion. But it wasn't long before he arose again and wandered from the parlor to the bathroom to the kitchen to the hallway and back to the window, peering out at the snow. My mother and I watched him go through these paces several times. It wasn't until years later I realized he'd been looking for Helen.

* * *

In the quiet stillness the rapping on the front door sounded like muffled thunder. Instead of getting up to answer it, my father and mother looked at each other as if to say: Who would leave their home on Christmas night to go out in such a storm? Still they did not get up to answer the door, as if the grown-ups were afraid they might be greeted by a spectre. And maybe they really were nervous about this possibility because my mother ordered me to put down my skates and see who—or what—was standing out in the snow at our front door.

Vaguely spooked by something in my mother's voice, I moved halfheartedly down the dim hallway. At the door I stared at its knob a few moments before twisting it very slowly, but a rush of snow-speckled wind yanked it out of my hand and the door slammed open with a loud boom. That crash, and what I found on the other side, chased all the scariness away instantly. "Aunt Harriet's home!"

Harriet, wound in a thin dark coat, fake fur collar raised, knitted cap pulled down over her ears, was flanked by a bunch of her kids—my real cousins. On the porch they stood snow-shrouded, cold-bound, weary-lidded. "Hiya Peter, Hiya Mary, Hiya Pavlos—come on in everybody!"

As they stamped their slush-coated feet and shook the snow off their coats and caps and mittens, muddying the wooden planks, I heard my mother in the parlor, with a strained voice: "My sister, all the way from Minnesota?" But it was when my father declared, with considerable volume, "Harriet!" that I realized why neither of them had come out to greet my aunt: Harriet was the only person in the world who could get my father and mother to screech at each other in front of me.

* * *

Whenever Aunt Harriet had had a divergence of life-views at home, she would show up at our doorstep in Brooklyn, a few kids within reach of each hand, a bundle or two at her feet, and a pathetic look in her eyes which meant she couldn't pay the cab driver. What really boiled my father's blood, however, was that once settled in, Harriet could not be "budged by a goat." Not until she had forced her husband to beg forgiveness or, much less likely, had spit out her pride and went back to him. Either way, this took months, and my mother and father battled—if not always with their mouths then with their eyes—from the moment they arose to the moment they lay down, and for as long as Harriet remained under their roof.

"She's always wearing my slippers!" my father would cry.

"Her feet are clean!" my mother would retort.

"She never does anything to help around here!"

For this my mother had no response. Harriet did not pick up her wet towels, did not help with the dishes, did not throw out the garbage, did not do anything but smoke cigarettes and gaze at herself in the mirror as she brushed her hair. Worse yet were the visits paid us by her husbands during these episodes. Some nights Harriet and hubby would rehash an extensive list of domestic complaints while I tried to do my homework and my father tried to read his Greek newspaper. In other words, his protests were not unjustified, but he never noticed that Harriet and her kids also brought lots of liveliness into the somber rooms of our house.

* * *

When my aunt appeared in the archway to the parlor that Christmas night, her dark hair wet and tormented by wind, with kids lined up in front of her like a protective shield, my mother shrank back into her chair and my father's face turned red as Santa's suit. I felt the muscles in my stomach clench as he sprang out of his chair, stomping toward my icicle-thin aunt and elfin cousins. I was afraid they would be trampled.

Looming like a storm cloud over them, he roared: "Stand over furnace grating, where the air is warm!"

My cousins inched into the room as cautiously as mice tip-toeing past a sleeping cat in a cartoon, finally huddling over the metal grillwork in the center of the floor, the hot air fluttering the edges of their hair. Aunt Harriet stood stone-still, speechless in the archway.

Staring directly into Harriet's eyes, my father said, in the softest voice I'd ever heard come out of those cracked lips, "Merry Christmas, Helen," his hands spread out toward the open gift boxes under the tree, the apples and pears in bowls, the ribbon candy in the narrow dish. "Come in so you can see beautifool decorations on tree."

My aunt, confused by his mistake, remained silent, but she set down the soggy shopping bags and moved slowly toward the open arms of the pine.

The Occupational Rehabilitation of Cousin Henry

In my family work is more than a means of putting pilaf in the pot or wearing out the minutes between 9 AM and 5 PM. In my family work is a patriotic service, tantamount to saluting the flag—the blue and white stripes of Greece or the stars and stripes of America—eight hours a day, five days a week. To say Uncle Stavros was lazy, therefore, would be to say he was a traitor. To say Uncle Kosmas worked like a jackass in his too-short life would be to say he died a good soldier. . . . This perspective should not be confused with the Puritan work ethic, which has its origins in an anti-Elizabethan, religious over-zealousness. With Hellenics it is an anti-Socratic bias, a political reaction against the good-for-nothing thinkers of pre-Christ Athens who sat around and talked, talked, talked while the city-state was crumbling under their flabby asses. No wonder Greeks in this century have gotten it into their heads that the only way to recoup the long-lost glories of their Golden Age is to work, work, work.

While the performance of labor is viewed by us as patriotic, the taste for work is considered hereditary. It was naturally assumed, for instance, that if Stavros had borne a son, or daughter when it comes to that, the by-product would have been a lounging-scrounging paragon of indolence. And when

Merrula's son, Henry, was old enough to take out working papers—my family thought it queer that one needed "papers" to do that for which we were created—it was naturally assumed he would begin setting up pins at the bowling alley on Saturdays; take on a break-of-dawn newspaper route; apply as an after-school mop-and-hop in the neighborhood florist; establish a modest but thriving mutt-shampooing operation to fill a free time slot between church and lunch on Sundays. And, all the while, do tolerably well with his grades in school. It was naturally assumed he would race into manhood suffering from an acute case of the narrow-sightedness that is the curse of the ambitious: unable to set aside enough time in which to enjoy the pistachios and figs which rewarded his numerous enterprises. . . . None of this—neither the profits nor the excesses—came to pass. Henry Tarsipias turned out to be the laziest of the lazy, far more accomplished at idleness than even his Uncle Stavros, an off-and-on, here-and-there handyman.

Henry's career in slothfulness began early, right in his own household. My cousin refused to take out the garbage, go to the stores for a quart of milk or loaf of bread, wipe the dishes, sweep the snow off the steps, collect the dirty socks gathering dust balls under his bed. But it turned out to be nothing personal against his mother or his younger brother Harry: He was the same way in school, and would've behaved lackadaisical in church too had he not stopped going on the grounds that it was "too much like work." Henry shifted from day to day the way most people shift their weight from leg to leg. Nor did he make any effort to acquire a trade for the future.

"Why bother?" he said earnestly.

"But after you graduate high school," his mother pleaded, "how will you live?"

"Same as you," Henry replied. "Pop's insurance."

Merrula bit her cuticles, watched for omens, and begged the family for advice. "Give him a good whipping!" seemed the consensus. But Henry, approaching sixteen, was already twice the size of his mother—north to south as well as east to west, and was given to unpredictable explosions of temper. Who can say in what manner he might've responded to the sting of a belt?

* * *

On his seventeenth birthday, after months of tug-o-warring with his mother—perhaps even with his father by way of the grave, Henry Tarsipias dropped out of high school. His rationale was that since he was a freshman—and had been for two years, books could only become progressively more annoying to him. Sounded logical to me. For though people who pour equations and grammar into one's waxy canals have been known to invent a tale or two about their students, I fully believed their reports that Henry had never completed a single homework assignment at Franklin K. Lane High. Of course the objections at home to his quitting weren't based as much on the principle that education is essential to a healthy, wealthy, and wise future as it was that his mother didn't want him parking his butt in the house all day, watching her soap operas, smoking her cigarettes, drinking her beer—while she was recording deposits and withdrawals of customers at the Emmigrant Savings Bank.

If Henry had trumped up a philosophical explanation for his lack of effort in or out of school (even that shop-worn complaint that life is pointless and, therefore, so is any kind of labor contributing to its sustenance), or if he had simply kept his teeth clamped shut, he might've drawn our sympathy, our forgiveness. But no. Brandishing a bramble of coal-miner's hair and squared-off lumberjack shoulders, Henry crowned his sublime sluggishness with loudly, regularly offered disdain for all those who were "dumb enough" to work for "mule drivers" at "dull-as-dishwater jobs" for "peanuts." "You'll never find me that hard up," declared Henry, sprawled out in an armchair, mashing peanuts between his sharp jaws, staring at the Yankee game on TV.

Such protestations notwithstanding, my cousin finally did go to work. But never let it be said he was not true to his bias. Henry became employed only because his total lack of patriotism weighed so heavily on the family's deep reservoir of guilt. Collectively we kept finding for him "things to do," plus his mother threatened to "kick a hole" in the TV tube if he didn't "at least try." I say "kept finding" because despite numerous opportunities at a variety of careers, of odd-and-end jobs, Henry exhibited a special genius for losing his way, his memory, his carfare, his temper, and, therefore, his position. It would not be cruel nor inaccurate to state that his only steady employment was getting canned.

First he was a table clearer/wiper at the Acropolis Cafeteria, owned and operated by Aunt Harriet's former paramour Christos, out on Metropolitan Avenue. No uniform or tablecloths, but at least it was with almost-family and at least he could eat all he wanted and at least it was not far from home and at least the salary was . . . well, the food was edible, anyway. But as tolerant as Christos can be, and that is nearly as consenting as his namesake, not even the Lord's Only Unbegotten Son could have been expected to dish out a salary to a peusdo-nephew who, his first week on the job, only showed up at 5 PM on Friday—the very moment that pay is handed out. Particularly since Henry got irritated when he found no payroll envelop waiting for him.

"I didn't come in this week 'cause I was sick," Henry sniffed self-righteously.

"We can't pay you for sick days when you haven't even started working," Christos pointed out in a kindly tone.

"So that's your game," said Henry. "Well it's against the law to employ a child without working papers–I'm gonna report you to the Labor Board!" . . . a threat he never followed through on probably because he was too lazy to find out where it was located.

Then he did some time in the shipping room of the blouse factory in which my mother had operated a massive black sewing machine years earlier—when the family's winter coat allowance had dwindled to a few dimes and nickels, mixed in with thin red bingo markers, in a cracked cup. The foreman still remembered Evangelina as punctual and steady. So her nephew was hired to fold the flattened cardboard into boxes, insert fresh blouses, tuck in the flaps and, finally, neatly stack the shiny white boxes in large tan shipping cartons. When Henry ran out of blouses, he was supposed to haul another batch on a hand truck up from the lower floor—a task too laborious for his lifestyle, he said later. Instead he would pack the boxes with garbage, of which there seemed an endless supply in a row of huge, nearby barrels. Receiving orange peels and scraps of cloth and used tissues instead of crisp white blouses in the boxes did not please the shops served by Greenpoint Modes. Not surprisingly they threatened to take their business to Astoria Togs, their chief competition. When the globe-shaped foreman called his new employee into his cubby-corner, Henry became indignant, attracting the lined-up eyes of the machine operators with his shouting: "Don't get your belly in an uproar! Nobody'd want to buy these rags anyway."

Through a friend of Aunt Delphinia's boyfriend, Theo, Henry went to work as a gas-pumper at a Texaco garage. At last, at long last it looked as though we'd hit upon the right placement for my cousin; his big ears and long nose seemed to sharpen around the roar of engines, the stench of burnt oil. For a week straight he showed up at the garage—and on time. That Saturday the illusion of occupational rehabilitation exploded, almost literally. Henry got into a squabble with a red-head, reportedly over her refusal to give him her phone number. So he had removed the nozzle out of her Ford's gas cap, pointed it into her window, and splashed gasoline all over her lap; then he took out a pack of matches, broke off a single paper match, and held it with his thumb against the striking surface until she—with, no doubt, a wildly shaking hand—scrawled out her phone, her address, her social security number even.

* * *

Relatives who dropped by the family headquarters in Flatbush always found Henry's vocational trials startling enough to cause them to rock their heads knowingly and to tsk-tsk their tongues hopelessly. And my mother gladly contributed a pot of harsh coffee, two or three stiff raisin buns, not to mention her eyes, ears, and mouth to the proceedings. But she got quite upset the afternoon her sister Merrula, who'd spawned the lazy oaf in the first place, alluded to the fact that Evangelina's only son–me!–had not invited her oldest son, my first cousin, to come work at the restaurant her semi-brother-in-law had founded. With a self-righteous squeal Evangelina replied: "God rest my husband's poor feet, he gave his life to keep that business up!" Aunt Merrula's plum-shaped face crumpled into a prune before our eyes, but at least she got the message: Evangelina didn't want the restaurant to go down the drain like leftover grease. I agreed heartily, though silently. I needed no help whatsoever in running that business into the sewer. Which is the reason my mother and I kept trying to pawn Henry off on other people's businesses.

* * *

By the time Henry turned twenty he had already gone through more careers than any three people are entitled to in a lifetime. In addition to those previously named employments, without a license to drive he parked and dented cars for Municipal Lots,

swallowed the donuts he was supposed to be sugaring at Kru-
gers Krullers, delivered—though not always to the correct address—urgent messages for Western Union, and dusted bones
at the Museum of Natural History—with nearly disastrous
results! . . . not to mention other endeavors that slipped by
our ears because they didn't last enough hours to have been
reported to the family at large.

Since none of these positions existed more than a week—
no, that's not true, he stayed on at Barney's as a barkeeper for
twelve days (he loved his brew)—Henry could not be said to
have gained on-the-job experience at any single vocation, not
counting loafing, a skill he refined daily the way a carpenter
works at smoothing his thrust with a plane. And the more
expert he became at doing nothing, the more irked the family
became. Personally I never felt particularly threatened by his
laziness . . . until one night on my way home after a wither-
ing day at the restaurant: I spotted my cousin in downtown
Brooklyn sprawled out on a bench as if it were a beach-chair,
whistling at the girls bouncing by, and it struck me that his
Floridian approach to life would enable him to live twice as
long as me.

* * *

Gradually the family let go of the dream of rehabilitating Henry
Tarsipias. To compensate for this loss of a receptacle for their
abundant concern, the family turned their attention on me—
their former ally, monitoring my love-life with the idea of aiming me toward some "nice Greek girl." But I can't blame them
for losing interest in Henry. It was no fun nagging a twenty-
something-year-old foot-dragger upon whom, it had become
thunderously obvious, they were having no effect. Curiously,
when Henry noticed they had begun shifting their focus,
interrogating me about Babs Sleat, a buxom Jewish divorcee
I'd begun to "see," my cousin looked as though he felt slighted.

Over a Thanksgiving roasted lamb at our place in Flatbush, beneath the hung-from-a-chain domed fixture which hadn't glowed in years, my cousin exclaimed: "How come no one tries to help me find a job any more?" Too stunned to reply, we watched and listened for clues of what that statement could possibly mean in the perverse mechanism of his universe. But all he did was sulk the rest of the holiday.

To my knowledge the matter did not come up again for months, and everyone more or less forgot the sullenness, the self-pity of Henry. In part they forgot because Babs and I were still getting together, despite the family's subtle hints and, finally, outright threats to cut me off—not from my inheritance, which consisted of a set of dishes and utensils manufactured in Greece, but from my "flesh and blood." But my cousin had been at work behind the scene, as we soon found out. Unbeknownst to us, the good-for-little had landed himself a position, or so Uncle Augie claimed. Seems Henry had been palling around with a group of fellows at the bowling alley bar, and they had taken a liking to him. He did, admittedly, have an impulsive, friendly smile.

"They gave him a lead on a good-paying job," Harriet's latest husband revealed, "and he's been at it three months."

"Three months!" we cried like a chorus of Sirens luring mariners onto the rocks at Scylla.

"Three months," Augie stated gravely, for it required repeating to be absorbed, and gravity to be believed.

"What kind of work is he doing?" we wondered with stretched eyes, suddenly willing to believe that life is full of tricks. Not that the sort of work mattered. It was work! But my mother and I were naturally very curious about any activity that could keep Henry showing up for a whole quarter of a year.

"Insurance," said Augie, sitting up straight in his dark-green suit jacket, just like a local insurance broker.

"In the actuary department?" I inquired with great interest.

"In claims?" someone else chimed in.

"No, no," said Augie, "in selling."

"You kidding?" I muttered. "I tried selling policies once and would've died from hunger if Alexandros Sr. hadn't gotten me into the food business. People always need to eat, as Papou used to say. Is Henry selling by phone or door-to-door?"

"He visits . . . companies."

I was impressed. "At the corporate level?"

"Well," said Augie, scratching his lotion-scented chin, "candy stores and groceries."

Before another used breath was returned to the suddenly close atmosphere in our kitchen, with a ceiling high enough to trap gallons of carbon dioxide, I understood the nature of the insurance being peddled by Henry Tarsipias: squeezing nickels and dimes out of neighborhood shop owners to "protect" them from the hoodlums for whom he worked. If the old folks didn't come across, some broken-nosed high school drop-out, too big for anyone's good, would put an inch-thick heel through a glass case that sheltered penny licorice drops or yellowed note pads. Next time, it could be a few bones. It's not as though these immigrant couples made any money. All they bought with their feeble candy bars set out on sagging wooden shelves was an illusion of freedom, unpacking and stacking and figuring and sweeping sixteen hours a day, seven days a week, while five percent of their dusty stock was swiped by customers who were also being robbed by their employers; and ten percent of their take was tithed out to two-bit thugs . . . small-time human beings like my cousin.

* * *

Henry Trasipias' regular employment revived the family's interest in his vocational development—and steered their eyes away from me! Understandably so, for his job offered just enough conflict between morality and patriotism to put the family to one of its most meaningful tests of character. There arose two basic attitudes: (1) This business of Henry's was evil, (2) at least it was work. When stacked directly one against the other, there is no question that point (1) took precedence over point (2). But if, in the ongoing discussions of Henry's fortunes and future, these two points were widely separated—as they often were, so that comparison became moot, or even silly—then there was plenty of sentiment riding on point (2). Surrounding a bottle or two of wine or whatever, they occasionally argued into the night in our kitchen. Since I had to get up at 5:30 AM to prepare for breakfast at the restaurant, I usually bowed out around midnight, but not before I had taken the stand. While I strongly favored point (1), I could sympathize with Augie and my Cousin Pavlos who held that this was "just the beginning;" that at least Henry would get to know the feel of work; that before we knew it, he would get on track with employment better suited to his talents. Exactly what those talents might be, however, never came up.

The patriotism faction proved to be correct in one respect: This was just the beginning; unfortunately, it was not the beginning of what they'd hoped for; it was the beginning of a long, successful career in hooliganism. Henry truly liked his job, and it's not difficult to see why. Ten, maybe eleven hours a week he worked—at fifty dollars an hour! This enabled him to move into his own four-room apartment on the Grand Concourse in the Bronx, having been assigned to the courthouse area, near the Stadium. Furthermore his visits to the candy stores and deli's and shoe repair shops and neighborhood pharmacies over the first several months had never required anything more strenuous than a smile and a square, open palm on the counter. At least that's what we heard from Augie, who sometimes traveled to the Bronx on business— wholesale distribution of some sort. In a few ways Henry's position was like his old Western Union job—moving from place to place, but with one important difference . . . at that company he'd been a lowly deliverer; in this operation he was a big-shot collector. Thus his assessment of the working world had proven out for him: "Only stiffs work a long, hard day for coolie wages." Add to that the touch of prestige—the fright of shrunken, scrawny folks; the awe of curly-haired brats on tricycles; the long-lashed winks from counter girls—that came with his work, like tips, and it was understandable that he would seek advancement in his profession, like any up-and-coming executive.

* * *

Certainly attempts were made to "talk to Henry," partly to get a handle on his thinking, partly to let him know ours. And on at least one occasion a non-phoned-in, mother-to-son appeal was rendered. Henry could not resist the lure of her legendary, Italian-style spaghetti sauce. He took a cab all the way from the Bronx to Brooklyn, thumped his brother Harry on the shoulder with a "Hiya, Kid," ate half a dozen meatballs, drank two quarts of beer, and complained repeatedly how small their TV screen was—while staring at it throughout his mother's speech. Harry, a shorter but less lazy version of Henry, said nothing to help our cause. He simply looked and listened, eyes wide. Merrula, as resolute and lean as a five-year-old maple, had to bring up the subject herself, and it ended like this: "I'm happy you've found work, little Henry, but there are nicer ways to earn a living. Jobs that will make your family proud."

Undoubtedly eyeing the time gleaming up at him from his gold-wrapped wrist, Henry arose and smiled broadly, like a minor league ballplayer who'd been asked to autograph a scorecard: "What's the family ever done to make me proud?"

There was a good answer to that—that the family had never done anything to make him ashamed, and that was something to be proud of. Aunt Merrula didn't think of that. After

Henry left the two-and-a-half room apartment, the pre-war brick building that had been smoothed off at the edges by decades of polluted atmosphere, she escaped into the bathroom to blot her eyes. When she returned to the table her younger son Harry said: "Looks great, doesn't he, Mom?"

That encounter convinced her relatives that without a husband to back her up, Merrula was helpless against the big, young thug. Which is why Uncle Augie, Aunt Harriet's husband, was beseeched to intercede. Now Augie wanted nothing to do with this assignment, but there was no question he was the right man for the job. Augie had been followed for years by whispered rumors about his own workaday comings-and-goings. In short, Henry respected him. At last Aunt Harriet must've done a "Lysistrata" on him for he agreed to try. But if there had been no such game as baseball, they might never have gotten together. For weeks, we were informed, Augie had tried to lure him with beers and burgers to the Blarney Stone. No luck. It took a pair of box seats, Yankees vs. White Sox. Wearing a sharkskin suit and Stetson fedora, Henry elbowed through the hot dog-and-peanut parade, the hero-worshippers, the ticket-hawkers, arriving on time under the smooth cement facade of the Stadium. But even though the sky was clear, and even though the Yankees were winning by three runs, nephew and uncle could not agree beyond the ballfield. No surprise to me. Augie's task was a delicate one: He had to do an about-face on years of family brainwashing—he had to talk Henry out of working.

Right after the Yankee shortstop slapped a ground-rule double, and the roar of the fans had subsided, Augie commented: "A young guy like you shouldn't be working so hard—he should be having fun."

Henry's broad, easy face must've puckered into a serious glob: "I am having fun."

Gazing at the sharp creases in Henry's shiny suit, Augie

wound up saying: "Money isn't everything."

"It's not just the money, honest. It's like the family always said—work makes a guy feel like a big shot." I can picture Henry, at this point, inspecting Augie's satiny shirt, crocodile shoes, and adding: "Isn't that why you went after the quick kill, Uncle?"

Years passed before it occurred to me that Uncle Augie's mission may have failed for a much more basic reason: He didn't really try. I suspect Augie had gotten him the job. Augie may have been his boss!

* * *

Half a year passed and, according to patchy dispatches from the front-lines in the Bronx, Henry was dressing snazzier every day and talking more like a big shot every week. This may well have been the case—we never got to see him any more. The higher he climbed in his profession, it seemed, the less he wanted to do with us. I figured it was because of the nature of his business, but I came to accept that this would have been true of him even if he had worked as a locksmith. But if we did not get to see Henry's patent leather shoes and silk ties, we got to stare at the bunched-up skin around the eyes of his "customers," or people a lot like them. Curiously, even though our neighborhood shopkeepers were not those visited by my cousin, we felt increasingly uncomfortable entering the dim caves of their shops, chatting with Mr. and Mrs. Epstein, Mr. and Mrs. Lugden, Mr. Hornberg, and old man Brovurst, all of whom had given us free weather reports or an extra slice of bologna for years. My mother found herself walking seven blocks further just to pick up a pound of onions at an over-lit, overheated supermarket, where teenaged checkout girls in stained hair shoved the pennies in change across the counter at her.

While Henry's visits undoubtedly distressed his Bronx clientele—their dried faces already wrinkled into an acceptance

99

of life's unjust taxations, at least he'd never had occasion to flex the muscles that had formed on his body so firmly despite his lack of physical exertion. Or so Augie had assured us. Even if that were true, we all knew the line between belief and action, like the line between life and death, is very frail and often difficult to distinguish. We all knew that if he had not shaped a fist against the old, or uprooted with his knee a shelf nailed up to display slightly soiled greeting cards, it wouldn't be long before that temper of his got the best of someone. And that of course was true of everything . . . it wouldn't be long before each and every one of us saw in our minds less and less of the linen handkerchief in his lapel pocket, the meat-eating smile. And once those images faded from our heads, it wouldn't be long before we stopped speaking his name.

Gay as a Greek Wedding

My cousin Peter is as gay as a Greek wedding, and I am as straight as the spear that pierced Achilles' heel. But growing up in a family-sheltered enclave in Brooklyn, back in the 70s, I didn't know the difference until I was ankle-deep in my teens. Even after I had developed suspicions about sexual alignments in the world at large, I never imagined that a member of my own bloodline might be capable of turning upon his own gender. By the time I was a freshman in high school, I understood that such predilections can spring up anywhere, like a single dandelion taking root in an otherwise homogeneous lawn.

That's how I thought in those years, long before gay liberation had stumbled out of the closet, eventually making same-sex couples not merely acceptable but downright fashionable in some quarters. Because my generation had resisted learning to live and let live—had not even tried to understand, my discovery about Peter rendered me angry for hours, terrified for weeks, distressed for months: angry he had betrayed the family, terrified I might later be cursed with the same inclination—he was two years older than I; distressed he was living a life which made it impossible for me to look up to him any longer. These intense reactions might have been avoided if only I had taken into account the eclectic desires of my ancient, illustrious forefathers, including no less a manly figure than Alexander the Great.

Having pretty much grown up together—he lived with us

periodically, whenever his mother Harriet was in-between marriages, I never paid much attention to Peter's development, any more than I did to my own. Whether Peter's hands had always embodied a certain grace, even when they gripped a BB rifle, I can't say; nor whether his laugh had always bounced out of a high arch in his mouth, giving it a remotely metallic ping. To me they were simply Peter's hands, Peter's laugh. It wasn't until somewhat later that I noticed, and attributed significance to, these traits. What I didn't notice until several years later was that my own laugh has that same metallic ping.

* * *

What I remember most about our shared youth is that Peter never used his age superiority against me. Rather he established a common ground between our levels. When I was fourteen and impressed by the bare-boned efficiency of lean bicycles, and my cousin was already admiring the enameled flanks of automobile fenders, he inspired a mutual admiration for a classy French motorbike in a neighborhood store window. "On a pair of wheels like that," he said, "a feller could go anywhere in grand style."

It was not his advanced maturity, nor his protective attitude toward me, that made me look upon Peter as a hero. Mostly it was because, at seventeen, he had pulled off the ultimate gesture of manhood: defied his mother and latest stepfather by bolting from their two-family house in Queens, and thundering under the East River in the subway with a knapsack on his back to set up his own life in Greenwich Village. True, that's only a twenty-minute ride on the IND subway line from Metropolitan Avenue. But he might just as well have sailed from Hoboken to Piraeus in the hull of a cargo ship, for I had never known it was possible to turn one's back on so many relatives, so much heritage.

In a few months the earthquake of emotion set off by his

decampment subsided, and the family began to draw upon its philosophical reserves: Peter's thrust out of the family fold was characterized by assorted aunts and uncles as artistic. Now "artistic" was a dirty word with them, translating to little more than a glamorized form of irresponsibility. At the same time, faint echoes of their ancient culture must've surfaced in their minds occasionally, suggesting a certain well-rooted consequence in the concept. It was better than thinking Peter didn't want any part of us. The family remembered he'd been scratching words in the margins of Classic Comic Books and on lined loose-leaf pages ever since he could sharpen a pencil . . . broken phrases he started referring to as poetry. These efforts had always been looked upon with an eyebrow of indulgence, the way "playing doctor" among children was looked upon: a necessary stage of development that would never amount to anything particularly damning. In this challenge to family authority, however, Peter's history of scribbling was taken to their collective breast, providing the minimum level of solace the elders needed to look a neighbor in the eye whenever this subject surfaced.

Ultimately it turned out the family was right—as it has been in so many things—about the place of poetry in his life. If my cousin continued to dabble with the rhythms and music of language, we never saw or heard of his verses coming out in print, and when he returned to Brooklyn for holiday festivities at our house, smiling but withdrawn, sharpened pencils, notepads and slim volumes were never in evidence on his person. These days he is co-proprietor of an antique shop on Bleecker Street. And out of the most eccentric assemblage of loose-legged tables and bottomless chairs and chipped china, Peter seems to extract a measure of that succor he sought to trap, and preserve forever, in poetry.

My first visit to his shop—to *their* shop, which they called Lost & Found, had distressed me almost as much as my original discovery about him: Everything reeked with the damp suddenness of mushrooms, a scent and sense that I ascribed not to age, not to disuse, but to what they were to each other. . . . The iron meat-grinder, its throat interlaced with spiders' webs; the dry, tan, leather jacket, cracked into a topographical map of mountainous terrain; the body-length, wood-framed mirror that was shedding its reflectiveness; a pronged, splintery workshop implement, the use of which Peter could not adequately explain. And of course that ultimate object . . . his partner Julius, with eyelashes that, for no sensible reason, reminded me of insect legs, and a doughy neck that seemed like the substance of love turned inside out.

When my cousin introduced us, I faced the stranger's baby-blue, V-neck sweater and, without offering my hand, said: "Hi, Julius . . . how's business?"

"To be honest, Alex, we haven't been selling very much. But we're going to see if we can do better by brightening up the place."

I did not say much more that day, wandering up and down the dust-coated aisles, trying to appear fascinated. But mostly I was confused, working hard to make sense out of the odd collection that had been left behind by the ghosts of other times, other places, and which had somehow ended up in a dimly lit, over-cluttered shop on Bleecker Street in New York City.

At last, flapping my hand in goodbye to Peter, I closed the door behind me and filtered through the humid streets . . . past still-drying canvases depicting shoe-box skylines and bowls of fruit in primary colors and glossy nudes with none of the blemishes that would've made them interesting. The unframed rectangles were leaning like men out of work against store fronts and the steps of brownstones, where the artists leaned, too, unshaven and unbathed, making a listless pitch for sidewalk trade. Staring at these oily by-products of the instinct for survival, I was trying to stop myself from thinking about Peter and Julius at home, at night, together. And after an hour or more of wandering parallel to gutters that had begun to stink in the rising heat, I managed to overcome those thoughts through a simple trick: by visualizing Socrates and Plato strolling through Athens, four hundred years before Christ, hand-in-hand.

* * *

It was a year before I entered Lost & Found again, setting off that tremulous brass bell hooked onto a coiled spring. By then my attitude had grown up a little, at least toward the tin-ceilinged shop, which had been reorganized in the direction of easier access and livelier presentation: A giant billboard from Barnum & Bailey's Circus blared silently at the door. Inexplicably I felt a certain affinity with the shop's somber assortment, as if the stilled clocks and flaking photographs were trying to whisper something about the function of the past in my cousin's realm. Most of the gathered objects were not drawn from his own childhood years. Peter seemed to be rummaging farther back in time, as if gathering evidence from his mother's youth, earlier times when life . . . through the tunnel of five or six decades . . . may have seemed less threatening.

As far as I knew from my own life, Peter's youth had been pedaled more or less pleasantly into the seasons that had opened before us. So wouldn't a savoring of his own early toys have provided a more fitting sense of security? His true father had been buried when he was five, and there had been two other husbands led home by Harriet during his coming of age. But Peter had several brothers and sisters. That he should go along so many of the same paths as them, as me, and come out at a different place on the map of human needs, remained a source of amazement.

* * *

The truth about Peter's life had been revealed to me one week after I'd graduated from high school. With an academic diploma curled up in my bureau drawer—not yet flattened and framed by my mother, I got to thinking about my childhood, about Peter—the hair-raising Halloweens we'd stirred up around Mrs. Rhinosos' partially boarded-up house; the bike safaris to Prospect Park; the games we played on my porch, when it rained, which ended in cheerful bankruptcy. And wanting to be admired by him for my scholastic achievement, I suppose, I ventured into the mines of the subway. Instead of rumbling past lower Manhattan, as I usually did—on my way to Yankee Stadium in the Bronx or the stone-lion-guarded library on Fifth Avenue—I disembarked at West 4th Street, strode up the metal-treaded stairs, and found myself in another country. Or at least another state of mind.

What everybody had always said about Greenwich Village in those days may well have been true: that its cultural cohesiveness had crumbled into an indistinguishable extension of urban mercantilism, that it had become overrun by "weekend bohemians" from Long Island and New Jersey, that its poets were really advertising copywriters hiding behind dark glasses, long hair, and dungarees, as we used to call jeans back then. But to me, having just disconnected my body and mind from the unrelenting geometry of a Brooklyn neighborhood, where people watered their square plots of morning glories with round hoses every evening, The Village was an exotic island, ugly and beautiful, that had always appeared precisely as I saw it that morning.

A soft mist hung over the ragged rooftops. I was confronted immediately by a brick wall covered with a vast mural of brown and white men and women extending their hands toward each other. Sheets of newspaper levitated on the wings of a gust kicked up by a passing bus spouting dark fumes. Crossing Sixth Avenue I noticed a left-over citizen curled up in the doorway of a liquor shop that was not yet open: No doubt he would be its first customer, assuming he'd managed to panhandle sufficient funds the previous night. A long-legged, pale, watchful woman stood on the corner, legs apart, sipping coffee from a paper cup. A boy in blue shorts was led past me by a terrier on a leash. Leaning out a ground-floor window was an icy-haired, wrinkled woman in a washed-out nightgown, her baggy breasts resting on the sill: I could tell she was alone in the world, and had been for a long time.

Along Greenwich Avenue caged shops gave off a reused odor that belied their surface claims to freshness—natural foods, natural crafts, natural shoes, natural jewelry, natural furniture. . . . Displays of goods in showcase windows seemed to be struggling for an identity: a sarong and sari boutique, French kitchen-wares, a Brazilian leather shop, a Far East spice store, a Turkish curio shop; it was as if being American in any context in this section of the city was a sure sign of the diminishment of one's spirit.

Heading down Bank Street I heard sparrows chirping mirthfully in the brittle-leafed trees. Brownstones were pressed against each other like lovers embracing on the street, brick facades reflecting rustily; their wrought-iron handrails looked oiled. Purple and yellow pansies overflowed out of a row of wooden flower boxes. Near the corner a red motorbike was chained to a NO PARKING sign. . . .

Up a set of loose stone steps on Jane Street I hopped, the pleas of the valedictorian, Selma Slakoff, still reverberating in the canals of my ears: "The world is yours, but you've got to go out and take hold of it with both hands!" The heavy downstairs door was not pushed all the way closed, so I was able to slip up to the second floor without announcing myself. I pounded on his metal-sheeted door like the police in a pre-dawn raid. In a few moments I heard the chain unlatch and the door opened. My cousin looked slightly startled as he stared at me, utterly incapable of speech. His wavy black hair was flat against his skull, his brown-rimmed eyes puffy. He was wearing one of those gauzy Japanese robes, a black and white lily pad print, tied with a sash, apparently with nothing underneath.

"Aren't you glad to see me?" I said, proud over having astonished someone fabled in the family for his cool head.

Peter glanced back into the room, then addressed my shoulder: "Sure I am. It's just . . . it's very early and. . . ."

I stood there showing lots of teeth, pushing the dark hair of the Dropouloses out of my eyes, expecting to be asked in. Then I noticed, behind my cousin, a hairy white arm extended off the edge of the mattress that lay on the floor, and out of the apartment came a male voice: "Who's at the door, Peter?"

As Peter jerked away and said, "It's my cousin," a rush of color filled my face, and his.

Staring at me with discomfort, Peter explained: "A friend is visiting."

I too felt uncomfortable, lacking the experience to produce a look that would conceal what I now felt, what I now knew.

"Everything okay at home?" my cousin asked vaguely.

"Oh sure. I only stopped by to say hello, and to see if . . ." to see what? "I only wanted to see how you're doing, and I wondered . . ." wondered what? I backed up. "Last week I graduated high school."

"That's great," Peter said, forcing a smile into his lips.

As I edged backwards toward the stairs, unloading a leaden adieu off my tongue, I saw a great weariness overcome his young, Grecian profile, like a man who'd just been declared guilty of a crime he hadn't committed.

* * *

By the time the subway stopped at the Kings Highway station, I was bearing the weight of a gratuitous self-pity. When I climbed up out of the urine-sprayed passageway, I took several deep breaths to clear not my lungs nor my nostrils but my heart. The morning's mist had transformed into a light rain, and I began walking home, capless, along the soiled streets of Brooklyn.

My mother, robust and rosy-faced, was bouncing about the curtain-swept kitchen with a pot in each hand, and it struck me as strange she was not experiencing the same discomfort.

The instant her speckled eyes got around to me she said, "What's wrong?"

"Just hungry." The mention of a need for food was enough to distract her from her original question.

Soon Evangelina inserted three thick slices of liverwurst between two slices of white bread, scooped homemade lemon rice soup into a bowl, and nudged me toward the table. And as I sat sipping milk from a heavy Horn & Hardart's glass, gazing out the side window at the rain dribbling down the slatted siding of the next house, she asked: "So how is your cousin *Panayiotis*?"

"Oh, he's doing good, Ma."

"When is he coming back home to live?"

"Not very soon."

"What is he doing?"

"What's he doing?"

"How is he throwing away his life in that place?"

"Who says he's throwing away his life? Maybe he's writing lots of beautiful poetry."

Evangelina raised her eyes toward the ceiling, her way of demonstrating that I had just confirmed the very point she was making.

* * *

That was as close as I ever came to revealing Peter's secret; our secret, for it seemed my cousin and I were sharing a mystery again, the way we had as boys when we impersonated pirates or detectives. But as I grew older, I began to recognize that Mother Evangelina and Uncle Stavros and Aunt Delphinia— others much wiser than I, had known about Peter's secret all along, and had simply kept it to themselves. Out of respect for my family, I'd felt obliged to do the same.

For several years, as far as I knew, I was the only one from our family who remained in regular contact with my cousin. And one brisk afternoon in October, walking along Bleecker Street on my way to visit him at Lost & Found, I laughed out loud at the absurdity of how all of us had continued to share this unacknowledged secret. We had sustained our silence so long, I concluded, because we wanted to preserve the family's idea of itself and, no doubt, to protect Peter too. Of course he didn't need our protection, and proved it the following month by showing up with Julius, unannounced, at the family stronghold in Brooklyn for Thanksgiving dinner. From drumsticks through pumpkin pie, neither of them bothered to hide their respect and affection for each other, and for the first time that I could recall the family seemed unsure of its own moorings.

Once again, however, the philosophical reserves of my clan were dredged up out of the depths of their distant, if poorly understood, past. Mothers and fathers, sisters and brothers, aunts and uncles, nieces and nephews—all of us spoke easily to Peter and Julius across the golden breast of the turkey, inquiring after their daily affairs, relating some of our own, and laughing heartily, genuinely, as the orange sun melted into the brown hues of a November evening in the County of Kings. My cousin and the love of his life smiled at us warmly, responded cordially, offered anecdotes like small gifts, and went on sharing a successful business and happy household, extending the reach of our family in its ever widening gyre.

Romance Among the Pagans

No matter how far I may wander, no matter where I may try to hide, the family Hestiakos will find me and bring me back to justice, which among my kind is a synonym for familial duty. . . . This truth was embossed on my soul as an undergraduate at the State University of New York, in Oneonta, where I had been spending time with one special girl almost daily. With Setsuko in my life the approaching exams did not press so urgently on the back of my neck, and I scurried across the campus, from Science to English to History, buoyed by the knowledge that no matter how badly the day had whipped me in each of these classes, she would be waiting for me in her room that night. Regrettably, news of this amorous connection somehow reached my family, and one Saturday morning in May, my mother Evangelina and my father Alexandros Sr. and Aunt Harriet and Uncle Stavros and Aunt Delphinia pulled into the dormitory parking lot in their hissing sedan . . . all of them withered by the four-hour journey, all of them determined to find out what was "going on."

Today their attitude strikes me not merely as out of date but laughable. But at the time, though I was growing up in a rapidly changing, youth-dominated society, I never fully got out from under the sway of their old-world morality. I don't mean to suggest the family is opposed to romance. They believe the pairing of males and females is essential to keep the fluids of life bubbling within us—either from arguing day and night as the couple tries to get used to each other's quirks or, after marriage, by maintaining an active "you-know-what" life, which is how they referred to coitus. In the late 60s and early 70s, at least in my family, the word "__x" was not part of our vocabulary, in Greek or English; even after the so-called "sexual revolution" had spilled over this land from Berkeley to Woodstock, they pretended it wasn't really happening, despite pictures in magazines of wild-haired hippies holding up two fingers—or sometimes just the middle finger—and the breasts of these baby blondes bouncing around under their tie-dye shirts. The fact that such pleasurable fittings existed between people was enough to satisfy my clan—they didn't see any necessity for calling these bodily connections by name. But while my family went along with these "friendships," or what we now call "relationships," they also had stiff ideas about how they should be conducted. And especially with whom. Screwing a non-Greek would've been considered dangerous to one's health, while marrying a non-Greek was considered one of the seven deadly sins. Number two or three, I'd say. So if you were dating (or what they called "foolin' 'round"), it had better be with a Greek—just in case the devil slipped into the works and you found yourself needing to rent a banquet hall quick.

In the present episode, not only was the girl non-Hellenic; she wasn't of a Western heritage . . . Setsuko was Japanese: a further complication, for though World War II was quite a few decades behind us, it had not fallen very far behind in the memory of many families, including my own. Harriet had lost an old boyfriend, Stavros the tip of an ear—or so he claimed, and others their innocence in that conflict. So their blood still roiled over the idea of sneak attacks and Kamikazes and the cry, in fuzzy-looking movies on late TV, of "Bonzai!" That Setsuko was born and raised in this country, and was more authentically American than my relatives, made no difference to them. And that she was as graceful as a fresh-cut yellow rose seemed to make it worse.

* * *

To say I was surprised when they climbed out of the patchy brownish vehicle is mild enough a description of my reaction to be a lie. Setsuko and I were camped under a sycamore on the quadrangle, studying for an early Friday end-term. And the hulking bodies of the family quintet, leaving a path of mashed turf in their wake, made me feel as if I'd been caught with my hand in the poor box. Setsuko sat as still as an ivory statuette, no doubt contemplating some biological truth. Her skin was reflecting the soft sunlight onto me, making my skin glow, too. Innocent as the morning, she didn't realize we were being raided by a pack of Hellenic hounds from the big city until they were standing before us, a gun-metal glare in their eyes.

"Hallo, son," said Evangelina, making it eminently clear which relationship counted more to her in this fickle world. And Delphinia compounded the offense by adding, as if I were a child, "How skinny you've gotten, nephew." For one awful moment I thought every one of them was going to cite their particular relationship to me. My father saved me that embarrassment by providing a greater one. Handing me a lumpy, damp, brown paper bag, he shook his head in Setsuko's direction: "Who's this?"

"This?" I said apologetically, as if Setsuko were a cheap replica of a classic Japanese vase, "oh, this is Setsuko." And I added, equally apologetically, "a classmate." The paper bag, I could feel, contained plums over-ripened by the heat, and I remembered an old saying that had kicked around in my head for years: *Beware of Greeks bearing gifts.*

"Wel-," Evangelina said almost to her, "come," as if Setsuko had just arrived, intruding on them instead of the other way around.

"Good morning!" Setsuko chirped.

"Studying the homework?" my mother asked suspiciously.

"Getting ready for a final examination," Setsuko smiled.

Evangelina's eyes grazed over the open book in the girl's lap and spotted a schematic drawing of the human body. "Ah ha!" she said.

* * *

Only too well did I understand my family's tactics. As long as Setsuko existed apart from them, while remaining in contact with me, she would be considered a threat. But if they could look her hard in the eyes, and at least make it seem as though their judgments were based on first-hand appraisals, then they would be on the road to neutralizing her importance in my life and, therefore, in their lives. Or so they imagined. And when they witnessed the end result of their undermining—the dislike in the victim's eyes, then they would have confirmation of their original sentiments. "See?" they would say. "We told you she was no good."

The younger the aunt, the more honest the objection to a particular romantic connection of mine. Merrula, had she been there that day, would have said outright that the problem with "this young thing" was that "she's not one of us." Her older sister Harriet knew I would reject such a reason, so I knew she would preface her objection by stating, "It's not that she isn't Greek. . . ." And the first-born aunt, Delphinia, equally determined to prevent me from making of my life a shambles, would start out with a positive comment: "She's cute, but. . . ."

As for Evangelina, no one has ever accused her of being subtle. Along the way of accumulating her fifty plus years she had decided that being a Hestiakos/Dropoulos gave her the right to ignore, hell, to run right over any outsider. Wearing one of her immortal house dresses, the black print crowded with white ferns, she stepped close to me on the crew-cut grass and said, "We drove two hundred miles to see you. Put your books away and show us where is the coffee," as if Setsuko were not even present, as if she'd never been born.

"Setsuko," I said, my face flushed, "my family has driven a hundred sixty miles, would you mind if—?"

Without looking at Setsuko, my mother cut in: "She don't mind, son. Get your books and we'll go put some meat on you."

By now they had me surrounded—by their minds as well as their bodies. Since this was my first year away from home they still felt as if they owned me, and I guess I believed that, too. I began stacking my books. Setsuko, the sweetest girl who ever exhaled in any hemisphere, graciously gathered her charts and notes. Off she went, her pale orange skirt fluttering like a butterfly taking leave of its cocoon.

"See you later," I called after her. She turned and, with cheerful onyx eyes, waved goodbye. My heart jumped out to her. *I'm sorry, Setsuko.*

"You no have time to see her later," said Aunt Harriet.

"I'll see you later, Setsuko!" I repeated louder, though she had floated past the smooth-stoned gymnasium, out of hearing range.

"What kind name is that for girl?" Mother Evangelina demanded. "Sounds like medicine for . . . whooping cough."

"It means 'faithful child,'" I said, truly appreciating that derivation for the first time.

* * *

The weighty back door of the Plymouth was hauled open by Uncle Stavros. Between my father and mother I was obliged to sit. I felt like I was going to be rubbed out. Stavros started up the engine—on the fourth try, and we pulled out from under a ledge of oily smoke. I needed to puff out some smoke, too. "What the hell do you mean by brushing off my classmate like that?"

To a person—even Stavros in the drivers' seat, they looked at me with crumpled foreheads, as if they didn't know what I was talking about. And it's possible they honestly didn't see what they had done.

"Setsuko happens to be a friend of mine," I said, "a close friend."

"Ah ha!" said Evangelina.

I reacted to that generalized condemnation like a reflexive knee that had been struck with a steel hammer. "If I'm old enough to die in the war for this country, I'm old enough to decide who my friends are." Actually I'd been born too late to carry a carbine or M-1 rifle in either of the Great Wars "to end all wars," not to mention the Korean "Police Action." But ever since World War I, that sentiment had been a young man's favorite claim to coming of age in America, so I took advantage of that precedence.

"Girls are different from friends," Delphinia explained. Just beneath the surface of all they were saying, of course, lay this question: "How far has it gone between you two?" With such information they would know just how far they would have to go. That unexpressed question filled the car like a point of law can fill a courtroom. The car sputtered and staggered between the wide-waisted maples, which were leafing again . . . even as people in both hemispheres were still mourning their war dead.

Pulling up to the Seneca Diner two miles from campus, the six of us stomped through the chrome-covered front door like a motorcycle gang. A few locals and college kids were leaning over Cokes and burgers, smoking and chatting. I was thankful none of my pals were in sight. No, I wasn't ashamed of my family, their bagginess, their loudness. How could I be, knowing it wouldn't be long before I would be every bit as baggy, every bit as loud? I just couldn't take a chance on what my mother and her sisters might say to—or ask!—my friends about me and Setsuko. My Papou commandeered the large corner booth, and I was slid in toward the center, three women on the inside of me and two men on the outside.

After the order of egg salad and tuna sandwiches and coffee and Cokes had been coded on the waitress' pad, the trial picked up where it had been adjourned in the car. But I wasn't worried about the outcome, for times were changing all around them, and they would be forced—whether they liked it or not—to change along with them, eventually. Besides, I loved Setsuko, and there is no testimony on earth more compelling than love. Of course I had not taken into account that my family claimed the same defense.

"How long have you been . . . foolin' 'round with this girl?" asked my mother.

"Look, we're good friends and there's nothing you can say or do that will change this fact of life."

"Facts of life?" Aunt Harriet mumbled.

"We'll see 'bout that, you young sniper," said my father, speaking not so much out of personal conviction as to avoid being berated by my mother on the drive back for not saying anything.

"Alex's all grown up," Delphinia's tongue flapped, as if siding with me. "If he wants to be seen with a girl from another . . ." *planet* was the word she was looking for. . . "if he wants to carry on with a . . . Chinese, that's his business."

"Setsuko's Japanese."

I might as well have hit them in the face with a bucket of decomposing mackerels. Papou moaned, "It's against the law to marry a Jap!"

"Who said anything about marriage?"

"Listen, my son," said Evangelina, a sage terror shimmering in her flecked gray eyes. "One day you're holding hands; next day you're rocking baby carriage with twins."

"We've only been seeing each other four months."

"Holy Mother of Jesus!" cried my mother, her voice attracting the eyes of kids in the diner.

Said Harriet gravely, "Four months, a lot happens between

a boy and girl in four days, much less four months."

Yeah, I thought, *especially if your name happens to be Harriet.*

My father started digging nervously in his short-sleeved shirt pocket, pulling out a crumpled packet of Chesterfields. Without distinguishing between the two of us, Evangelina spoke first to her husband then to her son: "You're smoking too much . . . your family just wants to know—"

"I know what you want to know, and it's nobody's business but mine and Setsuko's!"

As easily as that they got the truth out of me. By sounding defensive, I had confessed that Setsuko and I were lovers. So distressed were they over this discovery that my mother pushed her twice-bitten sandwich away, my father crushed out his cigarette on the tabletop, and Stavros said passionately, "Don't you know you're helping the enemy?"

I started to explain that World War II was as dead as the monuments that commemorated the War of 1812; that Setsuko had been born in Rochester, New York; that her father was an exec at Kodak; that she had more right to be drinking Coca-Cola than they did. But it would have been a waste of carbon dioxide: You don't change others' bedrock convictions with mere facts. Abruptly lunch was over, all of them having lost their appetite at the same moment, and with Uncle Stavros proclaiming that only a Greek diner knew how to make "a real tuna fish sandwich." Like a jury about to debate a verdict, they arose as one. With an iron silence the bill was paid by Papou in balled-up one-dollar bills. The waitress, a lackluster brunette co-ed from Oneonta State, looked at us as if to ask, "Too many shells in the egg salad?"

Once we'd all gotten settled in the smoldering, plum-smelling sedan, Mother Evangelina broke the quiet: "You think we came all this way just to see how you're wasting your life? We all of us came here because we got big news."

I was supposed to ask what this news might be, but I just

couldn't give them the satisfaction. Finally Uncle Stavros wiggled his great moustache. "So tell him, my sister."

"You think I should?" said Evangelina to Aunt Delphinia in a tone meant to make me feel I was missing out on something important. And truthfully, by then, my curiosity had been stirred; yet I waited. She would come across; she couldn't help herself. "Ah," she said at last, "if you really want to know. . . ."

"If you don't feel like telling me, that's okay."

Evangelina flashed me her "ungrateful child" glance and proceeded: "You remember my cousin Katerina's younger brother-in-law Philip who lives on The Other Side?" (I'd never heard of them, but said nothing.) "This Philip, he has a daughter—very nice girl." My chest tightened. "Yes," she said as if I'd inquired over this amazing fact, "she's in New York City right now, and she's dying to meet you."

"Stop being ridiculous. How can she possibly be dying to meet someone she's never even heard of?"

"Oh, I wrote all 'bout you long time ago."

"You are too much."

"I sent your graduation picture."

Jumping Jesus!

"Alexandros Theodore," she began, the use of my full first and middle names grabbing my attention, "Philip and his wife Rhea, they want you and Galatea to get to know each other."

Galatea no less!

"Tell him everything," Harriet urged.

"My son, you and Galatea are engaged."

* * *

While I may be Greek to the bone, as my family claims, I've been on this side of the Atlantic all my life, so I'd never taken kindly to those who would appropriate any part of my life, especially my love life. When they tried that, they were entering an area that transcends mere nationality, trespassing on sacred human ground. It was time to assert, if not my man-hood—I had to be at least twenty-five to try that, or at least a spirited sense of self.

"Engaged?" I cried as we headed toward the wall of bricks that fronted the Student Center. "I don't want nobody interfering with my personal affairs. And I mean it! This is America. Your world is dead and buried."

That concluded the conversation partly because I'd hit them in their deepest selves, and partly, I realized later, because they knew that in two weeks I'd be coming home for summer vacation, back under their spell. By then I would have cooled off, they figured, and might even go along with the idea of meeting my "betrothed"—if only to shut them up.

At 7:45 PM they piled into the Plymouth, the road-weary shocks enabling the vehicle to sink within six inches of the tar. From the back side window Delphinia had the audacity to caution me about my behavior over the remainder of the term. "When you are promised to another," she said, "you can't be visiting with some little. . . ." It was particularly galling coming from her because she had married a Jew, only to become doubly evangelistic against intermarriage after divorcing him. Now all her romantic feelings were being poured into making hairdos at her beauty salon and saving me from "foreigners." But I knew that if I opened my mouth again, they would have climbed out and stood around advising me past midnight. Severely silent, I watched the car groan away from the curb, their leaden faces mashed against shatter-proof glass.

To escape having to tell Setsuko what my family had done to me—to her, I went drinking that night at a college hang-out on Chestnut Street with a couple of my dorm-mates, doing my best to keep up with them, beer for beer—plus a couple of vodkas for good measure. Long before I could solicit their advice about my romantic dilemma, however, I threw up all over the toilet seat, and swore I'd never get drunk again for the rest of my life. A promise, incidentally, I have not been able to keep.

* * *

Next morning, with a thick tongue and heavy head, I slicked down my hair and went straight to Setsuko's room to tell her everything. She was wearing a short-sleeved white blouse with a pastel skirt, looking like a living reproduction of a Japanese water color painting. "What happened to you last night?"

"My family annoyed me so much I had to go out drinking with the guys."

My honesty didn't seem to please her. "Things didn't go so well with your parents?"

Because it's not easy admitting that your relatives can stampede you into ridiculous circumstances, I revealed, "My family is crazy."

"They seem like good people," Setsuko replied, her wide, dark deer eyes aimed at mine.

I moaned over her gentle attractiveness, over the absurdity of what I had to tell her.

"What's wrong, Alex?"

"Nothing. It's just that . . . do you know why they drove all the way up here?" Of course she did not. "They drove four hours to let me know I'm engaged. Can you imagine that?"

Of course she could not imagine that. Setsuko, though born and raised in the Western Hemisphere, still managed on occasion to display a fully developed Far Eastern inscrutability. She sat in silence on the edge of her bed, weighing my words in her wholesome mind.

"It's all in their minds," I added. "I've never even met the girl. I don't want to meet her. It's these god-damn old-fashioned Greeks. They're crazy!"

Suddenly her inscrutability, flapping about us as delicately as a Japanese kite, broke away. "Didn't you say anything to them about us?"

"Yes, sort of."

"It doesn't sound that way to me."

Even though it was all nothing, merely an expression of my family's congenital over-bearing protectiveness, Setsuko looked hurt.

"Don't be upset, Honey," I said, edging closer to her on the side of the bed. "These ancient Greeks are still living in the last century. They'll marry you off, baptize your babies, and bury you before you can take off your shoes. It has nothing to do with the way I feel."

Setsuko shook her head, deeply mystified by Western inscrutability.

* * *

The last two weeks of the term had been crammed with catching up on our term papers, so there hadn't been much time to pay attention to the indefinable, yet unmistakable mist that had settled in between Setsuko and me. Now I am not one of your pretty boy, statuesque Greek gods. I do the best I can with matted hair, burnt-looking eyes, and sunken chest. Even if a few of my college buddies didn't think she was all that sparkling, the truth is I needed her much more than she needed me. And hollowed out by the knowledge that we would probably not be seeing each other for three months, I swore I would "come down hard" on my parents for butting into our love life. I would refuse to meet the girl.

"I'll write you all about it."

"If you can find the time," she said, looking at her toes, pale and bare against the floor.

"I'll write you every day!"

Setsuko kissed me softly, nodded stoically, and it was that image of her smooth, glowing face, upheld by dainty cheek bones, that bounced around in my mind as the Chevy—driven too fast by Danny-boy, my dorm buddy from Sheepshead Bay—cut a diagonal, southeastern slash across the state. I was determined to have it out with my mother and father as soon as I arrived. Why wait and risk wasting all that pent-up emotion?

In a few hours the coupe screeched to a stall-out in front of a three-story structure that had been held over from the last century, a house which didn't feel anything like home just then. Unloading my suitcases, paying my share of the gas, and wishing Danny-boy a wickedly hot summer, I marched up the wooden stairs, glanced defiantly at the broken-down love seat on the porch, shoved open the door with a clatter, and cried out aggressively, "I'm hooo—mmme!" The whole goddamn neighborhood, plus assorted relatives and friends and strangers, were crowded into the large living room. It was a party—for me! A gang of them rushed me as if I'd just come home from the war decorated with a Purple Heart, all of which derailed my single mindedness. All I could say to Evangelina, square and smiling at me proudly from across the room, was: "Jesus Christ, Ma!"

As I was shaking hands and forcing my face to smile and having my shoulders swatted, I froze. A goat-faced girl no more than sixteen, wearing a purple, too-long, bulky dress— obviously someone still smelling of the boat, had crawled up beside my mother. The peculiar twosome started making their way toward me through aunts and cousins and neighbors, and past Papou, who waved at me as he sampled an anisette. Instinctively I backed up and reached down for my suitcases. But it was no use. They would've followed me all the way back to Oneonta. Had my "fiancee" turned out to be a bull dog, I wouldn't have been surprised. Why else would they be so anxious to dump her off on me? But a goat! That was going too far! Nor had I counted on them pushing her into my arms so soon.

"Alex!" Evangelina called, "I want you meet someone."

Not since that scare of pregnancy with Setsuko had I prayed. I considered it now, but I doubted it would've done any good since God was probably in cahoots with them. Instead I tried to attract the attention of my boyhood friend, Lowell, hoping to get him to come over and spring me from this trap with his run-on sentences. But that fuzzy-headed traitor was having too much fun telling lies to my cousin Mary's golden, attentive eyes.

"This is my son, Alex," said Evangelina to the girl, a fine shadow of hair outlining her upper lip. "Alex, this is Astroscia, Galatea's sister."

"Al . . . lo, A . . . liss," she stammered, revealing dark gaps where her eye-teeth should have been.

Lord, there was more than one of these creatures in the world, and this had to be the younger of the two. Then the brat had the nerve to bleat-giggle, as if she knew a secret about her sister and me. Well, I had a few surprises for her—for all of them. Life was too precious to squander on a family of goats.

"When Galatea see you coming," said my mother with a young girl's elation, "she go upstairs to look in mirror."

"Seven years bad luck," I mumbled to the immigrant upstairs more than anyone else.

"Oh, look, here she comes," said my mother, pointing, and I looked, and there she was, stepping down the stairs in a bright blue peasant skirt and white fluffy shouldered blouse: a painfully fresh enlivening of Pygmalion's statue of the perfect woman—with crackling, sunshiny hair; creamy, smoothly sanded shoulders; peaches for the skin of her cheeks; and eyes the color of the Aegean Sea. If The Classical Age of Greece could've been personified in one young creature, this was she, descending into the room like the goddess of the mysteries of the heart. Galatea was love made whole before the senses.

I must've sighed out loud because the goat-faced sister bleat-giggled again, and my mother kept nodding with satisfaction, backing off slightly to open the way for Aphrodite. As I stared at Galatea wafting toward us, her hips rocking rhythmically like waves breaking against the shores of Mikonos, her eyes and mouth exuding pleasure, I could actually hear and feel my heart quicken under my breastbone. Around us the sounds of sprinkling laughter and cellophane crumpling and glasses meeting seemed to spiral toward the high ceiling and tie themselves into a huge bow overhead.

"My Engleesh not so good," she smiled without embarrassment over this shortcoming, her white teeth filling all the right places. "My name ees Galatea. You are Alex, yes?"

"From my folicules to my toe nails!"

Though she had not understood my tone or my words, she laughed with sounds that reminded me of wind chimes, and with a tempting pull to her full lips, bright without the assistance of lipstick. My mother was too delighted over my stunned facial expression, too smart to try to add anything to what was obviously taking care of itself.

* * *

What happened to my heart during July is difficult to explain. Setsuko and I had a wonderful relationship: Both of us tended to be more quiet than demonstrative, with an interest in biology that went beyond those gentle times when our bodies lay naked against each others. In spring strolls off campus, through a hilly stretch of woodland that we liked to think belonged to us, we had discovered a sense of ourselves and of each other which promised, over time, to reward us with true depths of feeling. And understanding. What's more, she seemed to like the way I looked. How much more can a short feller with misaligned teeth expect from life? To me all this added up to love. Yet from the moment my eyes had found Galatea in the world, and my nose had whiffed her imported airs of lilacs, and my ears had let in the music of her voice, I was lost . . . drifting rudderless in the wake of her essence. Not that I forgot Setsuko. I wrote to her regularly—not daily, but every few weeks, though I remained vague in my correspondence about certain matters. And thinking of Setsuko at night, alone, still warmed my body. But what I'm talking about with Galatea is *heat.* Whenever I was around her, flames seemed to leap up within my chest, as if it were a built-in private furnace. My mother kept asking me if I was coming down with something. And I was. . . . American or Greek or Japanese, we are strange creatures, are we not?

Over the summer my family never once mentioned Setsuko, as if afraid of reminding me she existed. But they wouldn't let me stop thinking about Galatea. Our families scheduled us to attend functions regularly together—a backyard barbeque at which Uncle Stavros swore repeatedly because he was unable to light the charcoal; a dinner at Aunt Merrula's to partake of her famous *mousaka,* during which Galatea's thick-browed parents raised a toast in honor of "young love," without looking directly at us; a family outing to a sole-scorching, elbow-to-elbow Brighton Beach, at which I got a much better view of the rest of my betrothed, my beloved. No doubt that eyeful of her, packed into a pair of yellow cups and a band of yellow cotton, was all part of the family's scheme. But I felt appreciative rather than manipulated. I only wished I could've been Homer for a while to properly immortalize the total Galatea. The best I could do was record in my mind that her legs and arms were smooth as sanded balsam; her hands and feet were delicately shaped as if by Phidias himself; her neck was gracefully arched like a swan's. Hell, her perfect face should've been appearing on the covers of national beauty magazines. What I liked most about her physically, however, was her nipples—they extended half an inch off her uplifted breasts under her tight cotton blouses, and I figured those munificent breasts would've been very uncomfortable to strap into a bra. Then I had the delicious thought that maybe she didn't bother wearing bras. Ever. Galatea was so beautiful the sight of her made me want to cry. And later, when we had our first opportunity to get away from the others, and speak privately, I did cry.

* * *

Under the boardwalk, both of us sunk to the ankles in warm beige sand, sharp strips of light through the boards dividing our bodies into segments, Galatea spoke in a mixture of English and Greek that was slow enough for me to stay with, and mellow enough to siren the ships of Mediterranean adventurers off-course: "I am glad we have chance to speak. Your cousin Pavlos says you have girlfriend at school. These old-fashioned people, they don't see the young wish to make their own lives today. I too have a boy, in Thessalonike. His name is Jason. My parents say he will never amount to anything. But we are in love. One day, we hope to marry."

Would that be Jason of the Argonauts? I thought snidely.

"I am glad you feel as I do," Galatea went on. "It makes this easier for us. But we must not say anything to our families about our true feelings. Not now. The old have a right to dream."

And the young, I moaned deeply, anciently, *don't we have a right to dream?*

Up through the slats of the boardwalk I peered, allowing a spear of sunlight to strike me square in the eyes–as if I wanted to burn out my pupils and never be able to see her again. Or better yet—to fry that element of human nature that causes one to overturn loyalties in the flicker of an eyelash, the stretch of a limb.

* * *

With August fading into September, flanked by Evangelina, Stavros and two suitcases, I met my dorm buddy, my transportation, on Flatbush Avenue. Quickly, before Evangelina could kiss my cheek again, I flopped into the Chevy beside Danny-boy and we pulled away from under a hailstorm of goodbyes. Over the wounds in the expressway's surface we bumped, through the double-lane, tiled tube under the river, onto the crumbling streets of Manhattan. Soon we motored across the strung-out sweep of the bridge. Finally we rolled out into the clear, where used-car lots and supermarkets and ranch houses were lined up as if waiting for something to happen, though I wasn't quite sure what that might be. These, too, an hour later, dissolved into a ramble of gathering hills and patches of woods and an occasional reed-infested pond.

Though it made the trip seem longer, I felt fortunate Danny-boy didn't feel much like talking either. Maybe he too, over the summer, had been forced to look into the machinery of his own soul. Minnewaska, Poutaukunk, Utsayantha sank away behind us in the road, the way the Indian braves after whom those points on the map were named had passed into history. In three hours and forty minutes we pulled onto the Oneonta College quadrangle, and I dumped my body and baggage out onto the walk. Weak-kneed, hobbling about under leaves already crinkled around the edges, I felt years, not hours older than when we'd left Brooklyn.

* * *

The next day was windy and rainy, but Setsuko and I had a happy, kiss-and-touch reunion at the foot of her bed, the wispy curtains swirling into the room as if pleased we had found each other again. The day after that, sunny and calm, we walked through our crispy woods north of town, and the day after that, cooler and quiet, we discussed our summer vacations over hamburgers at the Seneca Diner. I did not mention Galatea, and I sensed that she wasn't telling me everything either. Yes, we had picked up our attachment again, but it had not landed exactly where we'd taken off from. The angle at which we saw each other had been slightly altered, just as the sun shines at a different angle in different hemispheres, at different seasons. In particular I noticed we no longer seemed to possess the power to peer directly into each other's heart.

Swiftly October became November, and as our minds sank deeper into Psychology 102 and Geology 116 and English Lit. 246, that comfortable atmosphere we'd established between us began to diminish, as if announcing the approach of winter. And by December the warmth had cooled away to a thin coating of snow which had settled over the northern world.

My Father, a Philosopher in Love

My Papou and I never got around to talking very much, not about things that matter. Early on I didn't recognize the detours in our communication as accidents of circumstance, peculiarities of personality: his working day and night, my never knowing what to say when he did speak, his general uneasiness with language—English in particular. And especially my misunderstanding his true feelings for me: I thought he didn't like me. When very young I decided he felt that way about me because I wasn't really his son; that I had been dropped off on his porch by my real father, a poetic soul who was too poor, yet warm and loving, to take care of me. The usual, obliquely oedipal scenario. But if I grew less fantastic as I grew older, I didn't get any closer to understanding why he didn't care for me. So the silence between us enlarged. Through my teens, into my twenties the only time we spoke about anything other than food, weather, or work was when it was forced upon us by conditions beyond our control.

* * *

Suffering from an illness of unknown origin and frightening suddenness, my mother had been stretchered out of our house by two brusque men, one black and one yellow, wearing starched cotton jackets, green. Before we even thought to call her brother and sisters to let them know what had happened, my father and I found ourselves side by side in his high-strung

Plymouth, its cylinders churning calmly that day as if to prove it was destined to outlast the family it served. Bumping along from pot-hole to pot-hole behind the flashing red lights of the glossy white ambulance, through pale, stricken, September sunlight, we sank into our respective fortresses of silence—partly in deference to our history, partly in homage to this wife/mother of ours who'd been attacked by a massive pain in her back that had made it difficult for her to breathe. And when my father finally stirred the air with sound, I realized it was just an unconscious verbalization of his thoughts:

"One day she's scratching dirt around marigolds in the yard, next day she's carried out of her house by strangers."

His voice, low as thunder rolling over Sheepshead Bay, drew me out of my own maze of feelings and fears: "What's wrong with her?"

Alexandros Sr.'s shoulders jumped upward, apparently startled to hear another voice beside him.

"Do you think it's serious?" I persisted.

My father gave me one of those stares which functioned like words for him: Their definitions were determined by the width of the slit between his lids, the tightness of the muscles around the mouth, the configuration of the brows, and the context in which all of this occurred. This time his look was steady, furrowed, bleak.

* * *

The springs under the car's metal shell had lost their elasticity long ago, so the irregularities of the Brooklyn streets jolted us repeatedly out of our seats. But my father hardly seemed to notice; he had sunk to the floor of his thoughts like a bottom-feeding fish. And I wondered that day, as I had many times before, what he did there in the tank of his mind; what places he visited, which people he saw, what regrets he had, which arguments he carried on and on with his wife and who knows who else? After we had bounced along several more blocks, I learned the answers to some of those questions, at least as they related to my mother.

"Times like these the years come back to you," he said, though I still wasn't entirely sure he was talking to me.

Once he got started, he seemed unwilling to stop, and I was shocked by the flow of words from lips famous for having uttered so little in the days and nights of his life. But this time I was smart enough not to reply, listening stoically as he made the years come alive again: days of feasting at weddings and birthdays and Easters, as well as ordinary days I'd never experienced directly, or had lost somewhere in my head. It was as if the threat to his life's companion gave him the right to talk all he wanted, at last; and as he told his stories, I stared out over the residential streets that pulled by us on both sides: The trees looked uneasy, skittish; the top-heavy, two-story houses seemed propped up against their wishes, with garbage cans huddled along the curbs like galvanized representations of the families that filled them each day.

My father went on, surprising me with how many words he had saved up. "How angry she is the night I bring home a cat. 'Out of this house with that . . . that tail!' she hollers. 'I don't want no hairs in my lima bean soup.'" He mentioned the year the Christmas tree had toppled in the living room, causing my mother to lock herself in the bathroom and cry for half an hour; and the arguments between them over Aunt Harriet moving in with us; and a riotous outing to the Greek Independence Day Parade in Manhattan: "Ya-Ya made Evangelina's face red as a roasted pepper that day." Slowly but surely my father worked himself up to a summation for these tales, which stood out in the dust-speckled air of the Plymouth like black points on a map of their lives: "It is dangerous for a man to feel too much for a woman."

Only when we rolled onto the grounds of Brooklyn General—a brick state of mind that looked more like a state prison than a hospital, and pulled up short behind the ambulance, did it break through to me that my father's musings had been tainted with a philosophical air. Papou, who had not gone beyond the sixth grade in public schools, who had worked his way to America on a freighter out of Piraeus, and who'd had to work like a man from age ten onward—mopping floors in a funeral parlor, stacking boxes in a warehouse, unloading dairy products from trucks, frying eggs in a luncheonette, managing a cafeteria until, finally, running his own coffee shop; and all for the right to continue working too hard to get little more than a poor living out of life. Was it possible that he had not merely been silent all those years, but had, in fact, been silently philosophical? Was it possible that people—regardless of education or experience or inclination—could absorb through cultural osmosis over the centuries what had been left behind by its earliest and greatest thinkers? Was my father, at the core of his heart and soul, not a restaurant worker so much as a philosopher?

* * *

After I'd called Aunt Delphinia—hearing out her exclamations of surprise and distress at the news, then asking her to let the others know, my father marched up to the reception desk: a semi-circle of stained hardwood placed strategically in the widest stretch of hallway like a buttress to ward off the public.

"No word yet," said the hatless, crimp-lipped reception clerk in white, her bones lodged upright against the metal chair. "I'll let you know when I hear something," she added, shifting the flesh-pink message slips from the left to the right side of the desk: It was the third time he'd asked in ten minutes.

"What room is she?"

Stiffening, the clerk said: "Please be seated in the visitors' area."

"I can't sit still," he declared, "till I know where she is."

The woman, who was neither old nor young, did not understand he was simply seeking firm footing in a revolving world that had suddenly changed speeds on him. But she did recognize the volatile exasperation in his upraised shoulders, so she checked her list: "Dropoulos is in 312. I'll tell you when you can go up. Sit down, please."

Six feet plus, my father thumped slowly back into the waiting area, twisted his thick neck left and right, apparently in search of a higher authority, and then dropped his bulk beside me onto the bench, cracking the glue in its joints.

"Your mother, she don't like to be left alone."

At least he was talking to me—even if he wasn't making sense. "She's not alone, Papou. The doctor's with her. The nurse is by her bed."

My father crimped his bushy brows at me, and I understood.

"They'll be letting the family go up and see her pretty soon," I replied.

"Why don't they tell me something? What are they doing to my little sparrow?"

The sound of a pet name on his lips rattled in my ear like the loose drain pipe on our house in a wind storm.

"Taking her temperature, checking her pulse, that's all."

After eyeing the clerk at the reception desk a few moments, he said, "They got to be very careful. She's such a delicate thing."

In the course of my twenty-plus years I had never once thought of my mapou—stocky as a high school fullback—as delicate. My father had to be talking about someone else, and after some reflecting, I realized he was: about a woman he had married decades earlier. So what I'd been told about my mother on several occasions was apparently true. Evangelina had been a frail, pert, marble-eyed beauty! The leaden photographs flashed before my eyes over the years had never convinced me that the demure creature with the glowing skin and narrow waist had been one and the same with the woman who chopped onions with the speed and sound of a machine gun, who claimed the devil would steal my soul if I didn't receive communion.

"Years ago the young did not have to worry about where to live, who to marry. The father and the mother, they decided everything."

I'd heard something to that effect—that my parents' marriage had been arranged before they'd ever met, but the only time I'd given that any credence was when they'd seemed inclined to do the same to me.

"Well," I said, "it all worked out for the best."

"Your mother," he said, gazing at the steel-rimmed clock on the wall, "she didn't want to marry me."

It was not the statement but his syrupy self-pity that startled me. After so many years together, how could it matter anymore? "You sure changed her mind, Papou."

My father's face assumed an expression I'd never seen in him before, a severe creasing of parchment-like jowls that reminded me of the way tanned earth cracks during a drought. It made me feel ashamed, but like other things I saw and heard that day, I didn't believe what his face was telling me—that my mother hadn't changed her mind, that she had never loved him. Or was it simply that he, like me, imagined he wasn't loved?

"Papou. . . ." I wanted to tell him he was just upset because his wife was spread out on strange sheets, in pain. But verbalizing this thought would have been like calling him a foolish old man.

My father startled me a second time by reaching out and slinging his arm limply across my shoulders, his hand flapping in the air like a bird which, suddenly set loose, wasn't quite sure what to do about its new-found freedom.

* * *

Before I knew what was happening my father had pushed himself up out of the chair and was pounding toward the elevator. I sprang after him, squeezing inside the stainless steel box just before the doors snapped shut. I couldn't say anything to him because we were surrounded by half a dozen people, some of them wearing hospital uniforms. But as soon as we stepped out on the third floor, I said: "You can't do this, Papou!"

Without even glancing at me my father stomped down the hall, looking for his wife's room. Through ether-tainted air I followed not far behind, mumbling, "They're going to kick us out." He found 312 just as the doctor was coming out of it.

"You must be Mr. Dropoulos," said the doctor, closing the door behind him. "They called from downstairs and said I might be seeing you."

"I want to see Evangelina," said my father. "I want to know if she's . . . okay."

Though the doctor was not much older than thirty, his pale hair was already receding, as if it were a professional obligation to appear older and, therefore, wiser. With two fingers inserted into his stiff white jacket pocket, he replied: "Your wife has a kidney stone. Very painful, but nothing to worry about." Then he looked at me: "Your mother is going to be fine."

"Thank you" was all I could think to say.

Having expected the worst, my father's cast-iron face seemed to crack into hundreds of pieces before reorganizing into an expression of gratitude, as if the intern had personally been responsible for saving his wife's life. The doctor permitted himself a faint smile.

A nurse, positioned squarely under a painfully crisp, dinghy-shaped hat, with eyes that bulged like a lobster's, opened the door from within and nodded us into a room with two high-set beds separated by a plastic curtain held aloft by chrome

136

rings. One bed was empty. In the second lay my mother stretched out on her back. The features of her round face were drawn close together by pain, and she seemed disoriented by the stark white walls looking down on her. As we approached, one on each side of the bed, her eyes widened and settled on my face, which also has a tendency toward roundness.

"The doctor says you're going to be just fine," I muttered. "You'll be back in your garden before you know it."

My mother nodded almost apologetically, then her pinched eyes took in her husband's broad, alert, perspiring face. Once again he was unable to find the words he needed, but he was not at a loss for something to say: His massive palms cupped his wife's small hand as gently as they might a sparrow with an injured wing.

The Truth is Risen

Sit with two or more Greeks of an uncertain age at a table of American manufacture, brooding over a bowl of fish-head soup, and you're more likely than not to hear a tale of visitation from the dead. Especially if you've just returned from a two-hour Orthodox church service dedicated to glorifying Jesus' Resurrection.

Assorted members of several branches of the Hestiakos tree, buttoned up in ironed cotton dresses and brittle gabardine trousers, sat along one side of the table; while boys in miniature suit jackets and girls in pinafores with matching pocketbooks sat on the opposite side. But only those of direct descent, and with a patiently accumulated solemnity, and boasting at least half a century of sun, wind, and hail in their faces, were permitted by family canon to relate such a tale.

This time it was Evangelina, with an appropriately serious expression, who took it upon herself to enter these sacred grounds: "Last night I dream our house is crowded with family, and Mother Hestiakos is sitting right there on the couch"—she pointed at the lumpy green depository for fat asses—"wearing purple dress she saves for weddings and graduations and funerals." Evangelina, dressed in her best brown tent which she saved for major holidays, peered toward the archway that led to the hall that led to the porch that led to the world. "Off the couch she hops like sparrow, and out the door she rushes saying no nothing to nobody."

The children who were lined up at the table—actually three tables set end-to-end in the coffin-shaped living room—were more interested in rice-studded meatballs suited up in grape leaves than in the wanderings of the dead, so they busied themselves by forking these delicacies into their mouths while Evangelina spoke in low, reverential tones. As for the adult contingent, our hardened skulls nodded respectfully at Evangelina's words, each in accordance with his or her age, temperament, and sex: the men with convincing jerks of our heads, since it was expected of us by two thousand years of mythology to be forthright in supernatural matters; the women with brief, unassuming dips of their double chins, since it was expected of them by two thousand years of male domination to behave modestly no matter what they had personally experienced.

"Ya-Ya looked thin and green as a stick of asparagus, but the eyes . . . ahhh, the eyes." In my mother's vocabulary of sighs, "ahhh the eyes" translated into something like "a strange gleam."

"At the corner she stands, shaking her hand to hurry up the bus," continued Evangelina, her own eyes starting to gleam strangely. "Her old crocheting basket is hooked on left arm."

"Ya-Ya was going shopping," interrupted my pock-marked Cousin Pavlos, a feeble attempt to contribute to mythology.

"No, no—the basket is filled with bitter figs."

"Bitter figs?" Cousin Peter mimicked, his face rich with wryness.

"Something in Ya-Ya's heart soured every last one of 'em," my mother explained.

"How do you know they were sour?" Aunt Merrula needed to know.

"It's my dream, isn't it?"

"But figs are the sweet fruit of devotion," Aunt Harriet insisted.

"Silence!" Uncle Stavros threatened with warped eyebrows, causing Aunt Delphinia's eyes to shut tight and Peter's olive-smooth hands to flinch. "Evangelina, speak."

Evangelina peeked at her big brother with an expression

of demure gratitude. "Ya-Ya climbs into the bus," she said, "and away it flies in the air. Up over Brooklyn . . . far away to Queens. When the bus comes down on Jamaica Avenue, Ya-Ya gets out and starts walking under the elevated tracks." By this time, Evangelina's voice had begun to sail high like a kite that'd been cut loose, and I found myself thinking of Chagall's airy works.

"Doing a little sightseeing?" my father inquired, forking a slab of roasted lamb off the platter and onto his large white plate. His face, as wrinkled as the shell of a walnut when he grinned, stretched smooth the instant my mother glared at him.

With her knobby fingers spread flat on the spidery table-cloth that had been crocheted by my Ya-Ya, as if laying her cards on the table, Evangelina said with pruned lips, "Ya-Ya pushes open the gate to cemetery."

"What for?" Aunt Delphinia inquired, her eyes blinking rapidly.

"If you can hold your tongue a minute," Evangelina snapped, "you find out."

"Go on," Stavros encouraged his sister.

"Ya-Ya stops at a small headstone and shakes the figs out of her basket . . ."—it was so difficult to get the words out, she repeated the phrase to gain momentum—"Ya-Ya shakes the figs out of her basket . . . all over the grave of grandpapou. . . ."

Not one of the adults moved, blinked, breathed.

"And then, so help me, Ya-Ya kneels down on the grave and, with tears pouring down her cheeks, asks grandpapou to forgive her!"

"Eeeeeeaaaaaa!" a bunch of us exclaimed at the same time.

Though the children's attention had been distracted from the golden bread implanted with dyed-red Easter eggs only momentarily by the outcry, Evangelina, possibly worried she had already said too much, concluded abruptly: "That's all I remember."

More than a dozen grown-up foreheads, dented to varying degrees by what we had faced in our lives, grew darker and more creased. It was our way of saying: "Ask us to believe the butcher cut the price for leg of lamb in half for Easter, but never, never ask us to believe Ya-Ya visited the grave of her husband to ask his forgiveness." But while we may have been skeptical over certain details in her dream, way down inside I think we accepted the gist of it, as we usually do with gifts served up by the family's subconscious. For if we attempted to separate fact from fancy, or chose to look upon these verbal plots as fictional, it would only water down our souls.

* * *

The passing of grandpapou had preceded only by months the passing of Ya-Ya. In both cases the doctor hadn't been able (or willing) to pin down any specific cause—"a little of this, a little of that," Doc Boutrides was quoted as saying. "They lived long enough so what does it matter?" Grandpapou and Ya-Ya had been pushing eighty. With such a convenient proximity of death dates, the family was free to tell the neighborhood that the genial old couple had died of "broken hearts." It sounded better. Plus it was true. But not in the usual sense: It was not because they couldn't go on without each other. It was because they couldn't go on *with* each other.

Though my grandparents' bitterness toward each other may have been the only true passion of their lives, as Aunt Merrula once remarked, the precise origins of this passion were a total mystery to family and foe. That is why we were all quite curious about one claim made by Evangelina in relating her dream: Ya-Ya's asking to be forgiven. . . . Forgiven for what? The answer to that riddle surely would've helped us understand the collapse of their interpersonal relations. But without more to go on from Evangelina, and with sticky young minds lurking at the edges of our adult conversations, there wasn't much we could do with that skimpy hint . . . other than make up things in our heads.

We had been making up things about them for years. One popular theory held that their nastiness toward each other was simply the natural byproduct of two totally opposite-minded individuals having been flung together by fate—another name for parents—in The Old Country. Yet both first wailed for mother's milk in the same village, its little white-washed houses scattered loosely over a hillside in southern Greece. Both memorized the story of Jesus in the same stacked-stone Orthodox Church basement. In school both were disciplined with the same crooked stick, and on the same part of the anatomy. And both, according to official documents, were four feet eleven inches at the time of their marriage. Though the spirit had struck grandpapou many months later than Ya-Ya, they also shared the same approximate dream: to bundle up their heritage and carry it on their backs to America, imprinting streets of gold with their dung-crusted sandals. Undoubtedly each also shared the same disillusionment when they stepped upon the sun-softened tar of New York City and found that the street had left its imprint on them rather than the other way around.

When the family finally got around to accepting that the similarities in the environment and lineage they'd shared had failed to bring about positive results, it was suggested by who-knows-who that my grandparents' life-long combat had been the result of their being too much alike. However, there were problems with that judgment, too, since their personalities really didn't seem very much alike. Ya-Ya was high-strung, grandpapou low-strung. My grandmother wore bright colors, my grandfather somber cloths. Ya-Ya was explosive, grandpapou simmered. All of which meant we would have to adopt a more psychoanalytical outlook than was customary with us if we were ever going to understand their behavior toward each other. My Psychology 101 course at State, a few years earlier, didn't seem adequate preparation.

The secret of Ya-Ya and her husband Yiannis' extraordinary discontent lay buried in their respective graves. In accordance with their dying-breath demands, they'd been shoveled into widely separated cemeteries in Brooklyn and Queens. Beholden by family ritual to pass on their story, however, we were doomed to wallow in the shadows left by a couple who had kept their troubles to themselves. Probably they were trying to protect us. Just as we concealed the truth—that our grandparents hated each other profoundly—from the fresh-faced, precious creatures who, each Easter, were able to reach a little more easily the painted eggs in the basket. Those eggs, like the children who coveted them, had begun to change as well—from dark red, representing the blood of Christ, to the multi-colored pastels of a commerce hell-bent on selling more shades of dye.

* * *

The Hestiakoses believe that all human creatures must make the most of the imagination granted to us by God to explain, to enrich, to extend our quota of moments in this all-too-brief, yet glorious season on earth. But we must also remember, in relating family tales about my grandparents, that myths are quite different from lies:

Aunt Delphinia, having been involved in enough relationships to know better, offered this romantic anecdote: "When Ya-Ya was a young bride, she sang to him as she hung her husband's socks in the yard to dry, and he sang back to her out the open window in the bathroom as he shaved."

Uncle Stavros, usually too wrapped up in his own contemplations of the perfect mate to comment on anyone else's domestic felicity, observed: "Your grandpapou had the strength to carry a donkey on his back, but would never lift a finger 'gainst Ya-Ya."

Aunt Harriet, who had remarried yet again, this time into money in time for Easter and who had taken to fretting about the family's American assimilation, added this to our mythology: "Grandpapou used to read gossip columns in the *Daily News* out loud to his bride at breakfast every morning, and she would laugh and laugh."

Mother Evangelina, who loved more and who therefore went farther afield with a kind of ultimate myth, this time speaking directly to the children: "This marriage of your great grandparents . . . it was made on Mount Olympus."

And so on.

For the record, my grandfather detested the tongue of his new-found land, and never troubled himself to learn to read or speak it very well, accepting only as much of the language as pursued him. And Hades seemed a much more likely breeding ground for this bedeviled pair than the mountain where the gods presided. Still we continued to speak of them as more loving than Hero and Leander, for it is unseemly that two people ripened to wisdom—two people who were duty-bound by family canon to love one another, should carry such rancor to their graves, souring the very earth in which they lie. Besides, we were afraid this knowledge might discourage the children from embarking one day upon an adventure of human trust.

* * *

Tributes to my grandparents' love for each other might have flowed like wine all day and night if less than four feet of Cousin Henry hadn't stood up before his twice-filled, twice-emptied plate, looked straight at me from directly across, and said: "Ya-Ya caught grandpapou screwing their cleaning girl."

What astonished me and, no doubt, all of us at that Easter table was not that this too-husky-for-his-age brat should turn out to be a family myth-smasher; not even that a pre-puberty punk should comprehend the nature of the physical oaths between married partners; mostly it was that the little rat had made this declaration with the stiff-lipped confidence of one who stood firmly on the side of Truth. Worse yet, his younger brother Harry nodded vigorously in agreement, as if he too had heard the news of grandpapou's transgression.

The tongues of experience turned to bronze, as in that silence after Jesus announced to the Disciples that a betrayer was breaking matzos with them. From under fishhook eyebrows Aunt Merrula aimed horror-stretched eyes in her son's general direction, too mortified to look at him pointblank. But if our tongues had solidified, our minds were bounding like rabbits in a field over these questions: How had young Henry come across such a notion, and was it true? Since his statement had lacked the embroidery of myth, I found myself wondering if his father, in delirium at the hospital (after his speedy sports car flipped over on the Brooklyn-Queens Expressway), had passed on that hateful intelligence. Maybe my uncle had acquired this information fortuitously as he climbed the porch stairs of my grandparents' house one afternoon, unexpected. His eyes could easily have been drawn to the living room window by the glint of a carving knife in Ya-Ya's hand—raised too high for a kitchen chore, and by a look of terror on grandpapou's face, while a teenaged, long-haired temptress, stretched out on the couch, struggled anxiously to yank her underpants back up where they belonged.

I believed Henry. Not because of any "inside" knowledge of the sexual proclivities of my beloved grandfather, but out of a sensitivity to human nature that is my birthright: Only physical disloyalty could stir such profound discontent in two people who have promised to love, honor, obey. However, if my grandfather had been caught with his pants down, why would Evangelina have dreamed that Ya-Ya was asking her husband to forgive her? Is it possible Ya-Ya was remorseful for not being all the woman she should have been for him . . . or maybe she regretted not having been more forgiving in her life. . . . Unless

. . . unless Ya-Ya too had strayed, a thought which brought to mind the bald-headed Sardinian she had brought home one night, before grandpapou had emigrated to Brooklyn.

Whether his claim was true or not, this much we understood: Young Henry was a threat not merely to the reputations of a pair of family figureheads—who were in no condition to defend themselves, but to our brave heritage of myth-building. I say "brave" because it requires courage for people to take up the imagination as a weapon against our finiteness, our imperfection; to see the slightly soiled as pure and clean; to see death not as a dark ending but a bright beginning.

Though not all of us had such heroic tendencies, we were united enough in our convictions to agree that no individual—particularly not a forty-six inch American-born Greek without hair you-know-where—should be allowed to bring down who knows-how-many centuries of story-telling. So when I arose in a stained white shirt, divided down the middle by a yellow polka-dot tie, a roasted potato stuck on the end of my fork like the head of a club, I knew it was with their full support. Actually it was more than support: It amounted to a special dispensation, for I was in my mid-twenties, without a single strand of silver through my tar-black hair. Not that I was looked upon as more deserving than any other of my generation. My temporary ascendancy had occurred merely because the elders had been stumped by what Henry had said, and because my heart and mind were bestirred by half a bottle of retsina which, standing at room temperature, had started to taste like resin.

"Henry Tarsipias, I want you to listen carefully," I began, shaking the forked potato at him. "Before they passed out of this life, Ya-Ya and grandpapou were married fifty years. Maybe more. Do you have any idea how long that is to be married? Chances are you won't even live that long!" I looked over my living links to the chain of life; they were shaking their heads in agreement. "Now marriage is not always what it seems, or what it should be. Sometimes couples forget to share their deepest feelings. Sometimes they do things which violate their vows. This does not mean they have failed each other or their family. It just means there are Truths only God can figure out." I looked into my glass, but it was empty. "Ya-Ya and grandpapou brought into this world every one of you children feeding upon this Easter lamb. That is why we honor them. That is why you must never, ever repeat what you have said before us on this day in which the Lord is Risen. Whether true or not, it is a lie."

With Henry aiming a peculiar expression at me, as if trying to comprehend how truth could be also false, I collapsed onto my chair. Loaded down by what they had seen in their lives, the faces of my parents and aunts and uncles began to bloom—a row of Easter lilies they became, their tongues wagging like stamens in a breeze: gushes of gratitude that made me realize I had reached beyond my everyday powers, had dipped into an ancient reservoir of experience that had been available to me all the time, without my knowing it. With penetrating beams of sunlight magnified through the broad window across my face and neck, I didn't really care that Henry Tarsipias—indeed all these children of our new generation—had spurned the opportunity to learn the language of The Old Country, and therefore had not understood a word I'd said.

The Devil Loves to Roll the Dice & Play a Hand of Cards

Throughout his life my father never let more words than necessary escape his mouth, believing that "talk, talk, talk" was mostly a waste of time, energy, and good sense. If he had known more about Socrates, who had changed the world simply by talking all day long, he might've felt differently. In any case it was not long after my father had passed into that everlasting state of silence—leaving behind too few explanations and too many responsibilities—that my mother's sister, Delphinia, began coaxing me to accompany her to Bingo games staged every Tuesday evening at St. Demetrius. These semi-legal amusements—the State was cracking down on "gambling" at the time, but still tended to look the other way when it came to religious establishments—were conducted by the parish faithful with a reverence that suggested Bingo-embodied influences which went far beyond its simple boundaries. For example, I suspect my aunt was betting that if she could get me to breathe in some incense-flavored air, and to eye a few sacred relics in the church's basement hall, the Holy Spirit would look kindly upon me and cast away the moodiness I'd been wearing like a cape of resentment against Chance. Which was all well and good except that Delphinia didn't seem to understand that the devil loves to roll the dice and play a hand of cards, too.

After I had moved back into my family's massive abode in a peaceful Brooklyn neighborhood—so my mother wouldn't be alone, and to cut my expenses, she and her sisters had immediately resumed their old habit of bossing me around like I was a kid again. "Get up off your *dupa* and come play Bingo with me," Delphinia demanded.

"Never been much of a Bingo fan."

"Sure, you got more important things to do," she said, giving me a look of disgust as I lay sprawled over the sofa like a dead fish washed up out of Sheepshead Bay.

I reached for the copy of the *Daily News* on the coffee table as if, in fact, I did have something important to do, such as keeping up with what was going on in the world.

"That's yesterday's paper—stand up like you got a backbone and take your aunt to St. Demetrius."

It had been many years since I'd paid homage to the God of Bingo, a minor pagan deity that had joined the pantheon after thousands of Greeks had emigrated to America, escaping what had become of their once-great culture. And since I was especially depressed that night over what was going on at my father's restaurant in downtown Brooklyn, and with my mother away cooking dinner for her 85-year-old "girlfriend" Penelope, I really didn't feel like hanging around that ancient, former old ladies' home, trying to keep out of the way of my father's ghost. So I hauled myself up onto my feet and fetched my raincoat. "If you don't want to miss any games," I said, "we better get going."

Impressed by her own powers of persuasion, my aunt tugged on her kerchief, slipped her raincoat off the peg, and followed me out into the drizzle of a prematurely inked sky. Instantly we were surrounded by the kind of damp chill that can make even a crowded city street seem deserted. But she began cackling warmly in anticipation of a good night at the tables. "My hand was itchy this morning," she revealed, meaning that Demeter, the goddess of agriculture, might be ready to plant a little cash in her palm that evening.

Under the glare of a viciously revealing florescence in the bus—the grooves especially deep around the openings of her face, Delphinia overflowed with the snippets of tradition and mythology that made the actual games all the more rewarding to a seasoned player. Emulating the silence my father had perfected, I gazed at the ad above the bus window: a photograph of a mousy brunette from Staten Island whom bus riders had voted "Miss Rheingold Beer" for April. As we rumbled closer to our stop, however, my aunt's chatter locked in on one point of local Bingo history that irritated her: "Last fall Birdie O'Brien comes in late, plays a coupla games, walks off with $900.—the jackpot!"

I couldn't help myself: "Guess God likes Irish Catholics better than Orthodox Greeks."

My aunt stared at me so hard I could feel tips of icicles pressing into the side of my face. "You don't understand," she assured me. "Birdie takes money from St. Demetrius and drops it into the poor box at St. Mary's."

Though there seemed nothing wrong with the idea of Greeks helping to support the Irish poor, or vice versa, I managed to refrain from saying so. But she had stopped talking altogether, so when we climbed down from the bus I tried to make up for my insensitivity: "I got a hunch you're the one who's going to win big tonight."

That prediction immediately distracted her from those darker thoughts, the upward pull of her cheek muscles visible even on a street where the light was tangled in spidery branches and telephone wires. Now her expressive, khaki-colored face slipped into a meditative mode: "How much, Alex? How much am I gonna win?"

"A few hundred at least," I declared without blinking, as if my information had come direct from Mount Olympus.

* * *

Delphinia's eyelids were still fluttering excitedly—her thick mascara breaking off in chunks—as we passed through the pronged iron gateway that had been put up, or so a deacon had told me as a boy, to discourage visitations from the "dark prophet." We pushed our way into the side door, and marched down the stairs with enough clomping of wet shoes to let them know, down below, that the games could begin shortly.

At the entrance to the hall a pair of powdery white faces, filtered by black veils, greeted us not with words but evenly weighted, solemn nods. It seemed to me I'd met up with these faces years ago, and that they had been veiled in black even then. Was it possible they had experienced a death in the family on the occasions of my only two visits in nearly a decade, or were they mourning everlastingly over the mere fact of death? The veiled ones sold us Regular (cheap gray fiberboard) and Special (cheap pink and green paper) Bingo cards, six for my aunt, two for me. Once the cash had been handed over by Delphinia, and had been tucked into their metal money box—a yellow crucifix had been painted on its cover as if to discourage thieves, we were allowed to pass inside.

Long and narrow, the parish hall was blessed with sturdy, if warped plank floors that had survived a couple of major floods, one dispensed by God, one by a lousy plumber. A few of the ceiling panels had been damaged by rain, too, and wherever these white rectangles adjoined, an optical illusion of crosses took shape. Curiously, the water stains had surrounded these inadvertent crucifixes like golden halos. Along both outer aisles stood two stolid radiators hissing valiantly against the dampness of the early spring evening, but several seated women were still wearing their coats. The hall was packed with more people than attended service on Sundays, not counting Christmas or Easter. But Father Nick would take them any way he could get them, any time of day or night, and had obviously been successful in luring lost and found souls into hallowed walls through essentially impious means.

Not used to seeing a young male in this subterranean district, three lumpy ladies eyed me suspiciously as we moved into the hall along the side aisle, passing beneath a row of pictures depicting Jesus patting the heads of children, sheep, cows, or horses. Midway down, at a table dominated by the upright posture of my aunt's friend, Mrs. Crousious, Delphinia halted, cracked a smile, and flapped a hand at her. I stopped too, but didn't smile, or wave.

"Saved a place for you, Delphie." Now, aiming her eyes at me, Mrs. Crousious added, "And you lucked out—there's a spot open right next to me." As she patted the wooden seat where she wanted me to park my ass, she showed off her cigarette-stained teeth.

A baggy-throated middle-aged woman with dyed yellow hair, camped one seat past the empty chair next to Mrs. Crousious, pointed at my head: "Look at all that thick black hair!"

"Leave him alone," advised Mrs. Crousious. "He's too young for you."

The ladies around them giggled.

When my aunt plopped down like a sack of potatoes at the eight-foot table—one of those pipe-legged, plywood plateaus which stand as the practical counterparts of the sermon—I squeezed sideways between the tables and sat down directly opposite Delphinia. But I was separated only by inches from Mrs. Crousious and the woman with the yellow straw on her head.

"How're you doing, young man?" said the straw lady, in Greek.

"How should he know?" Delphinia declared. "He just got here."

The woman sneered at my aunt, as if to say, I wasn't talking to you.

The stiff exchange between the women served to remind everyone that they had serious business ahead of them, and they immediately began to set out their Bingo markers or to study the numbers Fate had handed to them on their cards. Looking along the table, I could see their porcelain-white faces lined up like plates to be broken by baseballs at St. Demetrius' building-fund bazaar. Events to raise money for a church community center had been held annually ever since I could remember, and still there wasn't even a hole in the ground for a foundation. From the depths of her black pocketbook Delphinia pulled a tin cough drop box and handed it to me: It was filled with hundreds of green plastic markers, with a couple of copper pennies and blouse buttons in the mix.

Now my aunt peered blankly across the hall, as if she believed it would bring her bad luck if she looked directly at the raised stage up front before it was time to play. That platform supported a pair of card tables with folding chairs. Centered on the left-hand table was the wire cage which contained wooden balls with a number imprinted in red from one to 75 and preceded by one of the letters in the word "Bingo." On the chair at this table sat the Caller, a layman in a dark blue suit which, at certain angles, appeared to be as black as Father Nick's robes. The Caller's round eyes scanned the room with a proprietary gleam, like an actor counting the house.

Centered on the right-hand table was a pitcher of water and a glass. On this chair sat a woman who seemed to be wearing not a dress but a mud-brown umbrella, the metal ribs of which were apparently helping to keep her back straight. She, or someone like her, had been stationed there even when I was a kid, but she had never done anything (as the Caller sang out the numbers) except hand him a glass of water and peer over the crowd like the mother of a crooked councilman up for re-election. Having become more acquainted with the ways of the world, including the church at large, I suddenly understood her true purpose: to make sure the Caller did not somehow manage to fish numbers out of the cage which happened to be printed on the cards fanned out in front of his pals.

* * *

As the time for the first cranking of the cage drew near, the chatter smoothed out to a low, steady buzz. I detected a sense of anticipation in myself, too, but it was not the result of gambles I'd be facing in these games so much as those I'd been up against in real life. Having studied geology and literature at the state university, I had planned to go into teaching not out of a commitment to filling young minds with useful information but to enjoy three months of vacation every summer. Unless you were willing to dig in at one of the "death camp" public schools of New York City, however, teaching jobs were hard to come by. Taking the easy way out—or so it seemed at the time, I began "helping out" in my father's restaurant "until something comes along." Nothing did. And when my father collapsed in the middle of the lunch-hour rush, his business fell at my feet like a loose brick off a building in downtown Brooklyn. Since the brick hadn't hit me on the skull, killing me instantly, I bent over and picked it up.

Before I'd had time to acquire the basics of running a restaurant business, that brick had become an integral component in the wall of my life—the means of sustaining not only my own needs but those of my mother and Uncle Stavros and, in general, upholding the house which sheltered, in one way or another, the entire family. Then, without comprehending how or why, I fell far behind in paying salaries and grocery bills, and the workers were getting angry—a cook with three children threw her apron in my face and slammed the door as she left. Suppliers were beginning to refuse to ship eggs, butter, milk, cheese, bread, ground-up beef—not unless overdue bills were "taken care of." Because my father had given his soul and, ultimately, his heart to keep the business going, I didn't have the courage to tell the family about my difficulties. Nor had I inherited the philosophical disposition, so abundant in Greece before the time of Christ, that might've helped me let go of the dented pots and pans and chipped plates.

* * *

Soon as the round wooden balls were heard tumbling around in the cage, the players straightened their backs, or touched a Bingo marker, or tapped the edge of their tables. St. Demetrius still hadn't gotten around to purchasing a microphone and speakers, considering them, I imagine, instruments of the devil, so any Caller worth his weight in feta cheese needed a pair of hearty lungs to perform well on this stage. "O-72!" he bellowed with astounding gusto, considering his slight build and how tightly his necktie was drawn up against his Adam's apple. But he looked too much like a Turk to be spouting numbers at a gathering of Greeks, his eyes underscored by half-moons of shiny, leaden flesh, his cheeks pocked as if by the point of an ice pick.

"B-15!"

A general groan wafted through the hall.

"G-53!"

Finally he'd called a number printed on one of my cards: I covered it with a marker.

Rarely out of touch with anything going on around her, Delphinia said, "Good boy," as if I'd had something to do with having that particular number hollered across the hall.

"O-60!"

Oohs and ahhs.

"I-23!"

"What good is that?" my aunt asked no one in particular, her cards still without a single red disk in place, not counting the Free Spaces.

More than anyone in the family, Delphinia was hooked on Bingo. Maybe it was because she'd always been a gambler: married a Jewish clothier, moved to New Jersey, became pregnant, and miscarried; not much later, she lost her husband, too, to an Israeli woman ten years younger than she; my aunt had immediately moved back to Brooklyn, near my mother and father; attended beautician school in the evenings, winning a steady livelihood that didn't depend on any man; but then she grew lonely again, and gambled on Cornelius and Theo and others no doubt, but could not love again, or could not find anyone to return her love. Or maybe, after putting on that wreath of weight around her middle, she'd stopped trying. Yet even though she'd lost far more often than she'd won, whenever the numbers rattled around in that cage in the church basement, she apparently came out ahead in a way that was too profound for me to understand.

"N-36!"

"I got it on three cards!" my aunt gushed, loud enough to make sure other players would hear. Shaking a cluster of the dime-sized, transparent red disks from the rinsed-out pomade jar she always carried in her pocketbook . . . the way a card-shark is never without his deck of cards, she snapped them down triumphantly.

"B-7!"

"Oh, no," Mrs. Crousious coughed, the fingers of both hands pinching Bingo disks. "I got B-8."

I too moaned disagreeably, trying to keep in step with the mood of the players around me and, really, throughout the hall, most of whom struck me as anxious to cover over the private tragedies of their lives with colored disks.

"N-42!"

I slid a marker over the number. "There's no stopping me now."

At first snapping down the markers seemed to distract me

from my private tragedies, as if the game's simple-mindedness had been responsible for loosening the tension. Certainly it couldn't have been the hope of winning ten or fifteen bucks for completing a "Straight"—a row of numbers without skipping a space—before anyone else. Not even the idea of big prizes—anywhere from two hundred to, much more rarely, a thousand dollars—stirred me; winning the Jackpot or a Special was in the realm of the Homeric, as far removed from that basement hall as the story of Odysseus slitting the throats of sheep as a sacrifice, enabling him to speak with the spirits of dead heroes in Hades. Besides, to get me through my secret adversity I'd need the kind of cash that one could only get a hold of by sticking up the First National Bank. But to the worn, somehow brave women gathered there, and the scattered, scaly-skinned men mostly along for the ride, those prizes must've been waiting in the night like promises of eternal youth.

"O-64!"

"G-49!"

Dutifully I played, and each time someone roared "Bingo!" I found myself needing two or three numbers to complete a Straight. Not even close by their standards. And, in truth, I might've been too embarrassed to cry out anyway, having come not to win a few bucks but to escape my father's ghost by chaperoning my aunt as she pursued her harmless addiction. Without even a mild doubt over the outcome of these foolish games, however, I began to feel restricted rather than liberated by the tautly pronounced numbers: It was as if those slow, shriveled hands around me had clamped onto the edges of my sleeves and pant legs and were holding me in place. And the knowledge that those hands had also been forced to do things they had not planned on in their lives gave me no relief.

"O-71!"

"What?" cried an alarmed, narrow-boned octogenarian two tables away, cupping his hand around his ear. "Say again, louder!"

A frown overcame the Caller's face, and he shouted, "O! . . . 71!" offended that the strength and articulation of his voice had been called into question.

"That's more like it," the octogenarian muttered.

Cranking the cage, his face tinged with color, the Caller allowed another ball to roll into the palm of his hand. "B . . . 4!" he boomed.

"And after!" exclaimed Mrs. Crousious, and the age-old joke among Bingo veterans, by then having achieved the status of a common prayer, brought a self-satisfied chortle out of the crowd: They all knew it would be said; it was just a matter of who claimed the honor this time.

"B-11!"

Audible sighs.

"N-43!"

"These cards are no stinkin' good," Delphinia complained.

"G-55!"

More groans.

"I-19!"

"You don't look it!" spouted a man with portobello mushrooms for ears, his hand hooked over a cane, his smile broad as his face.

After several games of "Straight," "Round Robin," and the letters "X," "L," and "N," I had not even managed to win a little distraction. I felt edgy again, wondering if it might've been better, after all, to have stayed at home, working up the courage to tell my father's ghost what a mess I'd made of the leftovers of his life.

Standing up, I announced to my aunt, "Going out for some air," and scooped the damp raincoat off the back of my chair. "Back in a few minutes."

Everyone seated near enough to have heard glanced at me uneasily, as though I'd spit on those sanctified floors: I was cutting down my odds of winning by playing fewer games.

Though a band of worry had stretched across Delphinia's forehead, she tried to make up for my imprudence: "I'll play your cards while you're gone."

"Maybe you'll give me luck."

My aunt shook her head gravely. "The more cards you play, the more chance of missing a number," she murmured, revealing the flaw in their timeless tactic to get around the law of averages. "Hurry back!"

* * *

Walking heavily up the stairs through a passage of hand-plastered walls, I moved out from under the cloud of exhaled air, stale perfume, and perspiration that had saturated the basement. In this stairwell, oddly, the air smelled of the last church supper—beef and rice wrapped in grape leaves doused in olive oil. Instead of passing through the door at the landing which led outside, as I'd planned, I continued climbing the stairs. The scent of olive oil began to fade, and once I opened the door at the top, all those essences below were beaten back by the spice of candles and sweet wine and incense and whatever other mystical substances give a church its special claim on the senses.

Two paces inside the doorway I stopped, moving only my eyes as I surveyed the chapel. The left side drew its light—a muted glare—from the corner street lamp shining through red-and-blue-green-and-gold slabs of pimpled glass that depicted Mary watching over Jesus as a young boy. The right side was illuminated less brightly by tiers of flickering candles in what looked like short red juice glasses. Except for a soft hum from below, all was quiet, and the sanctuary was devoid of souls living or, near as I could tell, dead.

Soon I found myself stepping down the center aisle, and what I saw could easily have been the set for an old horror movie: the tall silvery tubes that implied subterranean sound, the shadowy replicas of Byzantine saints pieced in lapis lazuli in the concave ceiling, the immutable rows of Puritanically upright pews, which seemed to represent the consolidation of two great civilizations, one very old, one very new. Holding all this symbolism together was the altar, with its weighty metal implements of marriage, baptism, and death, including an iron incense shaker, a silvery spoon with curved handle, an ornate golden cup, and an inch-thick brass crucifix: These sacred devices lay evenly spaced across its thin slab of marble, over which was draped a runner of white linen with crocheted gold-threaded edging. Probably the handiwork of one of those ladies playing Bingo in the basement.

Propped up at the center of the altar was a gold-leafed, framed picture of Jesus Christ, in thorny headdress. The far-away look in His upraised eyes suggested He was peering into Paradise, looking for an explanation of what He was undergoing at Golgotha. A set of two steps, painted white, had been placed before the altar to permit children, as well as dwarfs, to step up and kiss the glassed-in face of our Lord. As a child, when I'd been led up those steps to kiss that blessed picture, all I'd been able to think about were the old people who had come before me and pressed their foul-smelling, crusty mouths against the same unwashed panel of glass.

Wandering to the front of the chapel, and looking over my shoulder to confirm I was alone, I stepped up on the platform and approached the altar. Up close I could see that what I'd suspected was true: The crucifix was made of gold—real gold. A poor church with thousands of dollars' worth of gold set out for anyone to see, to admire, to take. . . .

With both hands I lifted the crucifix off the altar, turning it around slowly, enjoying its smooth, glowing weight . . . and then I slipped the precious object into the pocket of my raincoat. Immediately I backed off and hurried up the aisle toward the front doors. Halfway to the exit my legs seemed to grow thicker, heavier, and I stopped running and stumbled into the pews, sinking down on the dark wooden bench.

Involuntarily my head drooped to my collar bones, my eyelids slid down. I let go of my raincoat and locked my fingers into each other. Like any person who prays only when he has fallen into hard times, I felt no shame at the sound of my voice sailing thinly into the scooped-out hollows of the chapel: "I don't speak to you often as I should–working too hard to get around to it." Now I began speaking not out loud but to myself: *For chrissake! You can't even be honest with yourself in church.* Taking a full breath, I peeked at the holy picture on the altar, closed my eyes again, then spoke quietly aloud: "What finally happens is I get lost in myself, worrying about succeeding or failing. But sometimes it looks as though nobody ever wins but the dealer. That's You, isn't it? . . . Don't mean to sound bitter, but I think You ought to know that when the odds are stacked too heavily against us, we're forced to lie, to cheat . . . to steal."

At some point I lost track of who I was speaking to—my heavenly Father, the saints, my earthly father, myself. All of us? But once I'd begun to dig the truth out of the black compost at the bottom of my soul, I was unable to stop: "The waiters and kitchen people haven't been paid in weeks; I keep telling them I have a big loan coming in, but it's not true—the bank turned me down. I lie to the dairy man and the butcher. I'm short-changing customers. And serving food that's going bad. Everything's falling apart, and I can't seem to stop it. . . ."

Blinking away a few tears in the dimness, I watched the candle flames swagger in unison.

"All I ask is that when You get around to looking over this mess, please take into account that I never wanted any of it in the first place—"

"Alex?"

Yanking my head around I saw the silhouette of Aunt Delphinia a few paces from the basement stairwell, her mass of wiry hair electrified by the shimmers of burning oil in a gilded lantern. With reflections trembling on her high Ionian facial bones, Delphinia said: "You won—you won the full-card Jackpot." While clearly excited, my aunt had not allowed her voice to become too high-pitched, too boastful, because she had entered sacred space.

I stared at the shifting shadows on her cheekbones a long while, wondering how much of my prayer she'd heard.

"Ehh! Didn't you hear what I said? You won a thousand two hundred and fifty American dollars."

I shook my head in disbelief.

"It's true I'm telling you," she insisted, closing in on me.

"Where is it?" I asked dully, cynically demanding proof. "Where's the cash?"

Delphinia glanced toward the altar. "You don't collect the big prizes on the spot. That kind of money is kept in a safe. Tomorrow you get it—I have to drop off a cake for the bake sale; I'll pick it up for you while you're at the restaurant."

For just a moment I allowed myself to think it was true, that Chance had spun the wheel in my favor for a change, that I had actually won a tidy sum of cash. Enough, at least, to keep a few promises until business picked up, or until the restaurant could slip away into a more honorable demise. But then my head went light, a side effect, I guess, of an even greater need to believe that confessions are heard, that prayers are answered if not by a host of angels, then at least through the human beings who love us.

"Let's go home," she said.

The Miracle of Uncle Stavros

Five hundred years ago in a village in Macedonia too small to have a name of its own, Hermes, the wheezing, retching master of the Hestiakos house, had his brother put aside a generous supply of wine, dried cod, pomegranates, figs, and gasped to family and neighbors gathered at his deathbed that he would provide a festive meal for the entire village on the occasion of his demise. Apparently having had last-minute doubts about the existence of a Hereafter, Hermes wanted to make sure he was not forgotten—at least too quickly—on earth.

It worked. His name, if not his face, lingered in the minds of villagers . . . for a year or two, anyway. But something much more meaningful had also, unwittingly, been accomplished: A ritual was born. The degree to which it was practiced over the centuries by different branches of the family varied according to how poor the people were and who was in power at the time. In general though it can be said the celebration has evolved—in the American vernacular—into quite a *blast*. These days no affair can compare to the burying of a Hestiakos for memorable feats of eating, drinking, dancing and, yes, loving.

Uncle Stavros, mainstay of the Brooklyn branch, was true to this tradition. True? He was fanatical about it. Three years before quitting this world he was clinking change into a washed gallon wine jug marked, "My Funeral Party," in red bingo crayon. And two years before his time he started penciling lists of food, drink, and guests on the wall beside his bed, which was lodged in what had originally been intended to serve as storage space in the uppermost gable of our three-story frame house. That was before Flatbush built all those garden apartment buildings without gardens, when the neighborhood still smelled like a town in Ulster County with an Indian name.

Never having married, Stavros had come to live with my mother Evangelina and me shortly after my father died. He told us he was moving in because we needed family around due to the departure of his brother-in-law. But we knew the real reason was that he needed family around him in the on-rushing years of his dotage. To outsiders he said he'd consented to move in only because the upright collection of boards and plaster reminded him of an Orthodox Greek church and was, therefore, a good place in which to wait for Judgment Day. Prophetic, he kept to himself the last year of his life, spending most of his evenings reminiscing in his room about The Old Country—even though he'd never been to Greece, having been spawned in New York.

By the time he released his grip on that invisible thread we call life, a dozen jugs of coins were causing his wooden floor to sag, and his wall was crowded with notations that resembled his own private, hieroglyphic code. Next day four of the undertaker's henchmen carried my uncle on a 4"x8" slab of plywood covered with a silky black sheet into our high-ceilinged parlor. Watching them, I couldn't resist the thought they were having a jolly time as they arranged my uncle on the folding table, which we had decorated with white crepe paper left over from one of Aunt Harriet's weddings. The table was stationed at the narrow end of the long room, away from the elongated hospital-style windows. One of the large panes of those windows, depicting St. Patrick slaying a dragon, had come out of the boarded-up Catholic church that used to welcome parishioners to its doors, before all the Greeks moved in and nudged the

Irish into another neighborhood.

Stavros' stubby, quaint body was then encircled by over-sized, cheap platters from Woolworth's overloaded with slices of beef cut so thin you could almost see through them. And there was red pepper-scallion salad, deviled crab, rice meat-balls wrapped in grape leaves, spinach pie, bowls of pickled beets and black olives the size of eyeballs, brine-soaked feta cheese in an immense bell jar—pita of all shapes and sizes and colors. And standing around on a separate table, like second and third cousins waiting to be asked to dance, were bottles of retsina, cognac, metaxa, ouzo, anisette, plus an assortment of American black and blue wines and pitchers of Rheingold beer.

No expense had been spared, no detail overlooked. It'd all been scrawled on my uncle's wall. That particular celebration was memorable, however, not for the avalanche of consum-able solids and fluids but for a phenomenon that was entirely unexpected. For the first time in remembered history a Hes-tiakos funeral party was blessed by a miracle.

* * *

Before the mourners could partake of that great spread of robust delicacies, from the smiling sardines to the frowning figs, we had to get the preliminaries out of the way—crying, but not for too long, on behalf of the departed; bragging about the fine things he would have done if he had lived longer; and discussing the cause and manner of his regrettable passing. In this case, however, most people were still not clear as to what had stopped that shriveled hand from scrawling on the wall.

After all, Stavros only drank liquor when he had some-thing monumental to brood about; refused to smoke even the mildest imported stogies; and was a life-long bachelor, so that couldn't have killed him either. Equally unclear—and much more important to us—was how my uncle had faced up to the final flicker, having turned his back on this life without benefit of an audience. In our family, rightly or wrongly, a person's whole lifetime may be judged by the way he spends his last few moments on the surface of the earth. Had Stavros turned chicken? Had he cried like a Turk? Or had he expired with dignity, accepting his fate like a true Hestiakos? These were questions that had all of us buzzing.

To Evangelina alone was my uncle's passing no mystery whatsoever, neither as to cause nor style. Several weeks before the event itself she had previewed her brother's death scene in a vision. At the time she didn't pay much attention to what she'd witnessed in her head, more or less believing her brother would live forever. But once it had definitely been established that he had stopped breathing, Evangelina became a sister possessed, describing that vision to anyone within earshot—and to several who were not.

Her favorite audience was her friend Birdie O'Brien, one of the few who managed to stay put each time Evangelina brought up the subject. One afternoon in our kitchen I heard my mother giving Mrs. O the unabridged version. At last she concluded fervently: "Stavros opened his ice and saw an angel of the Lord standing beside hisss bed. So my brother holy crossed himself, covered his nakit chest, smiled to show he was ready, and went back to sleep for the lasss time." The moral of her story was that my uncle had died with the decorum befitting a Hestiakos, and in holy circumstances.

Gentle but not gentile, Mrs. O, who was a Jew by birth, had only a marital interest in Christian angels. So each time Evangelina described that scene to her, she merely nodded at her friend's excited eyes. Besides, ever since that red-necked Irishman, Mr. O, had boxed both her ears in a family religious disagreement, Birdie O'Brien hasn't heard a word of gossip— nor much of anything else.

* * *

Throughout his life Stavros Hestiakos spoke kindly to cats and petted children politely. Cats and children made him feel closer to God. Unfortunately, he was allergic to cats and never had any children. There was no good reason for his allergy, but there was for his lack of offspring. "I never met the right girl," he would moan every so often. Truthfully my uncle was too thick-headed, not to mention too lazy, to get along with one woman for any length of time. But he never learned to hate, and that counts for plenty.

Because of his genuine concern for the fate of the family name in Brooklyn, about once a year he would brood heavily over his lack of a son. A daughter would've been okay, too, but in those days women gave up their own names upon marriage. The last of these sessions occurred one damp evening when I was working at the restaurant—and when my mother was helping to set up the spring bazaar at church. The scent of new life must've gotten into his nose, for my uncle unsealed a bottle of metaxa and took over the kitchen table. And by the time I got home from work he was drunk as Dionysus.

Seeing him slouched on the chair, and babbling to himself, I couldn't help chuckling. Sometimes I wonder if my laughter helped launch Stavros into his caper that night. While I was heating up some leftover breaded eggplant for his supper, he got up from the table, went upstairs, opened the window, and climbed out onto the roof of the house. And before I'd given any thought to what he was up to, I heard him through the open window, putting the women of Brooklyn on notice.

"You'd better sleep with one eye open," he warned them. "Stavros Hestiakos, he needs an heir!"

My uncle must've been in his late sixties at the time, but he almost didn't get a chance to plan his own funeral, wandering around drunk on the roof, proclaiming his fertility. I had quite a time getting him back into the house safely. Now looking back, I'd have to say that was Stavros' last stand: When a man loses his dream, it is the man who is lost. Once my uncle sensed his death approaching, he gradually forgot about carrying on the name. And by the time it was all over, there wasn't any sign of that commitment left in his creased forehead, his wiry gray mustache, his rusty teeth. Laid out in our parlor, he was truly alone in the universe.

* * *

With hunger and impatience growing, and minor annoyances—a fly on the leg of lamb—looming like acts of war, Evangelina stationed herself near the combination bier-banquet table and, with a brave, sisterly smile, began passing out waxy paper plates and flat wooden forks. Then she called out, in a voice too large for her body, "Come and get it!" which was as close as she ever allowed herself to become Americanized.

If it had been a Russian funeral the mourners might have hesitated to go up and pluck an olive; they might have worried that the deceased would open one bloodshot eye and look at them as though they were stealing from the dead. If it had been a Japanese funeral they all would've starved before tampering with the stockpiles of the Hereafter. But not at a Hestiakos funeral. Not with Uncle Stavros as the host. It was all there for the taking, all set out with love. Of course taking almost always implies some sort of responsibility, and a Hestiakos memorial party is no exception. When the mourners go up to the table to shovel some lamb stew and kidney beans onto their plates, and/or beef custard and collard greens soaked in oil and vinegar, they are also expected to pay their final respects and, at the same time, to thank the deceased for providing the life-sustaining meal they are about to eat. It gives the living a sense of humility, and helps justify that slight smugness one finds in a face that's out of the running.

The mass of relatives and friends and neighbors began

swelling and stretching, changing shape like a stirred-up crowd at a parade. Gradually a long, ragged procession was formed across the living room, along the hall, out the door, down the stairs, and onto the sidewalk: A lot of people liked Stavros Hestiakos. The line moved slowly, and each mourner glanced with solemn, humble eyes from the face of my uncle to a different delicacy on the table, spearing a slice of this and a chunk of that and a scoop of those. The spectacle of bowed heads and ravenous eyes was inspiring. I am sure those were very proud moments for my uncle, wherever he was.

Humility makes people very dry, so as soon as the first trooper—a honey-haired stranger who looked too Polish to be in attendance—made it through the front lines, they began to crack the seals, pop the corks. Quicker than a Brooklyn minute every mourner held a glass, and every glass was filled to the brim. And, often, over the brim—many a drab satin dress and shiny gabardine suit jacket was ruined at the funeral of Uncle Stavros. At first the drinking was quiet, social, sober, but then it took a turn for the better. Toasts ricocheted from one flower-papered wall to another, and I saw at least three glasses smashed against a window, a floor, a ceiling. In another hour there wasn't a face in the house that hadn't flushed bright orange—except for my dear, pallid Uncle's. But it wasn't because he was forgotten. At one point, stumbling up to his side, I poured him a metaxa. He never drank it, of course. But the living made up for this by drinking all the more fiercely, as if hell-bent on revenging some imagined slight by an outsider: We could not seem to stop. I think we drank that way to deaden our senses, trying in some small way to share Stavros' state of being.

By eleven o'clock not a soul could walk without an exaggeration of the limbs and trunk—from five-year-olds to eighty-five-year-olds. A stagger was even discerned in my mother, who'd been nipping quietly but steadily for the glory of her noble, silenced brother. In spite of her apparent festiveness, however, those of us who knew her best could see that Evangelina—another of those squat, olive-skinned Caucasians—Greek olives stunt the growth and turn the skin dark—was hoarding a worry in her vast chest.

The problem turned out to be pretty serious: Her sister Harriet had not shown up at the reception. Delphinia and Merrula hadn't noticed, or hadn't cared—not until Evangelina finally worked the annoyance out of her heart and up into her mouth. It was no excuse, she declared, that my aunt had moved back to Miami. Nor was Harriet forgiven simply because a platoon of her children and grandchildren and ex-husbands, most of whom lived in metropolitan New York, had shown up suited and dressed in darkish attire. Not even my cousins could say what had happened to Harriet. By not showing up Harriet had managed to offend the present and the past, the living and the dead. A host of our ghostly ancestors, led by Hermes, and distraught over her absence, apparently made a brief appearance at the party. Or so Evangelina claimed. Whether or not this established a family precedent I can't say. All I know is what my mother told me two days later—that she'd felt their hallowed presence around the banquet-bier and had practically seen their drawn, disapproving looks.

Powerfully aware she could not fully appreciate Stavros' reception until she met this responsibility head-on, Evangelina had wobbled to the liquor table and faced the floating, draped-over armchairs, or in some cases flattened-out mourners. As though making yet another toast, she raised her glass of retsina—a vigorous thirst quencher and emergency substitute for turpentine—and did her duty with a brief statement: "From this night on Harriet, you parrot, don't you dare call yourself a sister to me!"

My mapou delivered this proclamation loudly, as though she expected her voice to carry all the way to Miami; or maybe she wanted to make sure her voice would be heard in the next world. Whatever, she said the last word with such an impassioned twist of her thick waist that she knocked her feet out from under her water-heater-shaped black dress, and her bottom thumped on the floor like a sack of dirty laundry.

Instantly Evangelina was feeling better, as if she'd just finished reciting a long and deeply felt prayer. At the same time she must've wondered what her nieces and nephews had thought of her condemnation of their mother. Fortunately, one of the surest ways of being ignored at these family funeral celebrations is to go around making speeches, whether about politicians who are unfaithful to the people or relatives who are unfaithful to the name. It's likely cousins Mary and Pavlos and Peter and the others did not pay any mind to their aunt's rhetoric.

* * *

Dancing had broken out like a forest fire in one corner of the parlor. Funny-looking high-steppers in peculiar poses were raging from one end of the room to the other, attempting Greek, American, and assorted European routines. The action, stirring up clouds of cigarette smoke, reminded me of a stampede of wild buffalo in an old western. As the dancers grew more and more tired, though, they looked more and more like bow-legged goats working their way to the top of Mount Olympus. By 1:30 AM the radio station that had been providing the exotic, frenzied melodies of a bouzouki band was off the air; only a few stubborn stompers—primarily soloists—continued stumbling and shimmying to the electrical static which had replaced the music.

Those celebrants who were not dancing, or were semi-dozing, or were stupefied, had begun to cuddle up. Some neighbors criticize the amorous behavior at our funerals, calling it disrespectful to the dead. But love is the highest feeling we can aspire to in a lifetime, whether for one another or for the universe that is God. By holding onto and kissing and touching each other in the face of darkness, we let Death know we are not afraid, that love throws light even into the indelible shades of the beyond.

To my knowledge, the actual methods of expressing love in these rituals are not written down anywhere. Loving is considered too individual, I guess, to be regulated by decree. To one ancient duet loving meant humming romantic Frank Sinatra tunes while sunk halfway into our lumpy sofa—their heads so close the gentleman's hearing aid wire got tangled in the lady's hair net; down the hall I saw a middle-aged couple performing what seemed to be a fertility rite in the bathtub—he was scratching her bare back with a dried-out, claw-shaped root: mandrake, I presume; and the young had squatted in pairs, cross-legged, on the oval rugs and were passing the aphrodisiac—a blend of sake and tequila, sprinkled with an unidentified white powder, entering into the sphere of love more slowly, with more respect, and considerably more dignity than their elders.

Even Aunt Delphinia found herself a partner. Dr. Kazemis, the widower from Carnarsie, had had his eye on her for some time, and now he had an excuse to drag his folding chair next to hers. Intimacy developed quickly between them: They began sipping anisette from the same jigger. Unfortunately nothing ever came of this affair but, then, how could a beautician addicted to Bingo find happiness with an obstetrician who had no head for numbers? Sometimes, however, funeral romances result in more substantial connections. Two or three times Aunt Harriet announced matrimonial engagements just as a tribesman was being lowered into the earth.

* * *

To this day I can't figure out why that smooth blonde stranger started giving me the eye. I've never been much to look at—with a set of teeth that came in humorously crooked, and ears that grew to lengths well beyond the needs of hearing. Nor could she have started ranging toward my corner because of my rib cage, which seemed to have bowed inward instead of outward. The ways of the heart, I have since learned, must never be questioned.

Even though I must've been half a dozen years older than she—and therefore considerably more experienced and self-assured, I was intimidated by her beauty. I attribute this to the fact that I—like my father—was shy. But at least Papou had been tall. Anyway, before there was time to think of what to do about this challenge, I was confronted by her egg-shaped face and long-stemmed body—both of which I admired to an embarrassing degree. In the time it took her to lick her lips, making them shiny, I was in love. Wondering who had invited her, what her name was, if she had a boyfriend, if she liked short men with concave chests, and not wanting silence to come between us, to ruin a good start, I took a crack at her outer perimeter: "Are you a friend of the family?"

Ignoring my inquiry she wrapped her delicate, vine-like fingers around my hand and started tugging me across the room. There's nothing like a straightforward young woman— her mass of hair spilling onto her shoulders like honey-tinted sunlight, to shut a man's mouth. I followed her meekly and sat down on the floor with her, directly behind the table on which Uncle Stavros was flattened out. Who would've thought that this stunning youngish creature—I never did get her name— was destined to become the catalyst for my uncle's miracle?

* * *

There had been so much to do—people to invite, groceries to order, chairs to borrow, clothes to iron, furniture to polish, onions to chop, pastries to bake, potatoes to boil, salads to stir—that my mother never had a chance to think deeply about the implications of her brother's death. But getting away from the mob around three in the morning, resting alone in the kitchen for a few minutes, she noticed a clump of wilted lilies sticking out of a garbage pail, and I figure it was those forlorn flowers which provided that pungent reminder that Stavros was the last Hestiakos in Brooklyn. Not the last container of the blood, but the last bearer of the banner. Soon the only trace of that name would be on a modest tombstone, which they would poke into a patch of powdery Brooklyn dirt like an ice cream stick between a Chinese laundry and a Cuban grocery.

A sense of being utterly alone in the world—not as an individual but as a Hestiakos, rushed into Evangelina's heart and quickly overflowed, soaking her eyeballs in human brine. And it was this spilling over that enabled my mother to recognize she had to do something to save the name. Who else was there to carry it forward? Merrula never bothered about such matters, Delphinia was smashed, Harriet wasn't around, and my name was Dropoulos. But since Hestiakos blood was in my veins, too, I was at least able to sympathize with her high emotions in this matter.

The majority of the mourners were still concentrating on romance, with lips on necks and hands tucked into blouses and inside zippers. I was getting into the spirit, too. Fueled by a tankful of retsina, I had revved up sufficient courage to take a nip of that leafy ear beside me just as my mother splashed through the beaded curtain into the parlor. Her sobs were audible above the murmur of lovers: "It's not too late. It's never too late."

After zig-zagging through the tangled lovers and horizontal drunks to reach Uncle Stavros, my mother took hold of the lapel of his dark blue, cast-off suit jacket, and began her incantation in a low, vibrating, woozy voice: "Brother, I know you are tired, but I won't let you sleep till you find yourself a wife."

Evangelina watched Stavros for some sign. None was forthcoming, but she was determined. "Many healthy ladies have come to see you tonight," she declared. "You can take your pick!" By healthy she meant fat and ripe enough for child-bearing, and she yanked his lapel to show him she meant business.

My brain felt like a sponge at the bottom of the Aegean, and I was squinting at this mother of mine, this believer in ghosts and miracles, when the beauty next to me poked her pointy elbow into my ribs: She showed me a rope that apparently had been used to bind my uncle's body to the wide board on which he'd been carried to the table. Only after my mother had shaken the corpse, shifting the silky wrapping, did that rope become visible from where the youngish woman and I were sitting, snuggled against the wall behind the table.

Mother Evangelina's appeals became more and more urgent, violent almost, as if she were losing her grip on a drowning brother. "Wake up!" she cried, looking up his nostrils. "I am going to introdoots you to nice widow."

The louder her voice grew, the more annoyed the dim-eyed mourners became over having their loving interrupted; a few even took the trouble to swivel their heads in her direction. But the only person in the room who seemed interested in what was going on was the vivacious blonde beside me, staring intensely at my mother through green keyhole eyes.

"Rise up!" Evangelina demanded with sluggish desperation, "and take yooself a bride."

Before I fully understood what was going on, the blonde angel beside me had snatched a glittering knife from the table and cut the rope—my uncle's body sprang up to a sitting position and my mother, well, she fainted into a temporary death of her own, collapsing on the floor in a heap. I guess miracles can be too much even for believers.

The day his heart quit beating, Stavros had not been discovered by Evangelina until several hours after the fact. By that time rigor mortis had taken a stubborn hold on his legs, which were bent up toward his chest. (He'd always liked sleeping that way.) So Dybinski, a resourceful undertaker from Gravesend, had tied down Stavros' chest and thighs in order to straighten out his body, to keep it flat for the party. What followed has become a permanent part of family legend.

You never saw such a traffic jam: a Catholic stalled in the archway, an Arab stuck in a chair, a Jew in a window, an Italian in a closet, an Irishman under a table, an Armenian in a corner. Greek legs were spinning but getting nowhere. Arms were flapping as though trying to fly away. Huge red and white eyeballs gleamed everywhere. But the strange thing is that no one cried out, as though everyone had simultaneously lost the power to emit sound. Curiously Cousin Pavlos—who had slept throughout most of the ritual—was the first to reach the front door, as if in his sleep he had somehow known something supernatural was going on around him. He would not be party to any miracle, not a Polish Greek Methodist who was missing his eyeteeth. And once he made it onto the porch, they all gushed out of the place.

Although I saw with my own eyes how it had happened, the spectacle of my dead uncle, sitting up, grinning queerly, gave me goose pimples. And there must've been an awfully weird expression on my face, for the blonde was laughing so raucously she rolled under the table and disappeared behind the hanging table cloth. I never saw her again.

* * *

Though my mother did not succeed in digging up an heir, later she seemed quite content with the way things had turned out, having come to the conclusion, I guess, that a miracle was just as good as a namesake. A miracle, after all, was simply another form of immortality, perhaps more lasting than a name, especially in a world that has always welcomed a strange story into its safekeeping. Naturally that miracle became a big part of her life. If you asked her whether or not it was raining outside she would answer, "It was the most beautiful miracle I ever saw." Or she might even interrupt your conversation with someone else by saying, "Did you see the way Stavros smiled at everyone?"

Evangelina isn't the only one who believed in that fine miracle. Before they cleared out that morning, there were dozens of believers in the old converted abode. Considering the condition of the mourners at the time, and the doused lighting, this is not difficult to understand. What I can't figure out is why they continue to believe. Just this week I ran into Abdul in downtown Brooklyn, outside Junior's restaurant, and we got to talking about that famous party. Apparently he remains quite impressed by my uncle's feat, and I must confess I said nothing that might change his mind. I keep the truth to myself. I always will. If I didn't, it might get back to my mother. And it is my duty as a loving son to protect my mother's fantasies, especially at her age, especially since there are no more Hestiakoses walking the streets of Brooklyn.

O, How We Danced!

By American standards in the eighties I married late, by my mother's yardstick of family obligation, too soon. The evening I leaked my marital intentions, at cousin Mary's funeral, Evangelina had looked at me as if I'd announced I was about to commit a bodily sin in full view of family, friends, and undertakers gathered for the solemn event: "You got plenty of time for that, Son." I was thirty-four. If Gwendolyn had been Greek, even a little bit, my mother would've responded differently: "It's about time, Son." With the specter of a leggy-busty, Scottish-German, Presbyterian-Lutheran "chippy" looming over her realm of Mediterranean recipes, Orthodox dogma, and Brooklyn-inspired remedies, Evangelina scowled throughout the rest of the wake—at me, at the mourners, right into the coffin of her stilled niece, who's only act of willfulness worth mentioning had been to wander too far off shore at Rockaway Beach during a hurricane.

"Don't be upset, Ma. Gwendolyn and I are very much in love," I'd whispered amidst the velvety, desensitizing sweetness of too many lilies, too many charitable sentiments crowded into one dim, airless, casket-shaped room. But I should've known better: Our happiness is not what mattered to her. Of much greater consequence to all of them was the sustenance of the family's image of itself and, ultimately, their undying dread of diluting our Greekness any further. How could we possibly replace this current-day American civilization with ancient Hellenic culture, as my father had once claimed as his life's goal, if we kept getting watered down?

Evangelina had fixed her eyes on a spray of inconclusive light sifting out of a half-shell fixture cupping the wall, as if reflecting on aspects of love and marriage that her only son wasn't taking into account. My mother didn't share these reflections with me, but even if she had, it wouldn't have made any difference: I understood that "married love" could be experienced by no other means than plunging in up to your neck. Now, after nine years of being knotted emotionally, physically, not to mention legally, to Gwen, I have come to believe that marriage is a more or less continuous act of bravery. Who knows? Maybe that's all my mother had wanted to tell me.

Remarkably, on the precipice of her twenty-eighth birthday, my intended was still capable of an occasional blush. Sure she'd been involved with two or three—God forgive her if it was more—men. But none of them were the "real thing," she'd insisted, disparaging her ex's with a sharpness I found more disturbing than comforting. One evening however her past—in the person of an unshaven Viking in a hairy brown coat—bumped into us as we emerged from a movie house, and long after we'd left him standing on the sidewalk, Gwendolyn's eyes remained lit up from within. I'm not trying to make more out of that gleam than it was. It's just that her proclamations of "goodbye to all that trash" sounded tinny then, like a 78 rpm phonograph record of Al Jolson singing, "How I love ya!" The incident made me think that women never, ever let go of their earliest fondlings. In some primal way, it seemed to me, all women belonged to the first men who had aroused them, who had soothed those swellings in the hollows of their bodies. Yet another of the melancholy actualities of married love.

By my thirties I too had had my encounters with the opposite gender, though not nearly as many as I'd planned on. I blame this on my shortness and, especially, my shyness, with which I'd been afflicted ever since it became cruelly clear, in my early teens, that I was not going to develop Herculean biceps nor an Aristotelian mind. Nor were my dull eyes and limp hair likely to attract an offer from Hollywood. When you factor in these truths with the behavior of the women in my family—predisposed to keep their men off-balance with a get-ahead-in-the-world shoving forward and a religious-and-old-world tugging back—you can imagine the effect this had on a young male trying to find his way: I wandered through my high school years in a muddle, spending less of my mental energy on studies than on weighing the pros and cons of a life of celibacy. But it was too old a Roman Catholic idea to take hold in so young an Orthodox Greek. Besides, in my senior year at Flatbush High a girl/woman by the name of Teena Rolleck, who was more or less public property, took pity on me.

Except for one short-lived relationship and assorted dates at Oneonta State—where I'd studied geology, biology, minored in literature, and gazed wistfully at co-eds' tits and asses—my amorous encounters didn't amount to much until well into my twenties. But not before I'd paid heavily in emotional surcharges . . . the brunette who petted my best (and taller) friend's thigh throughout the movie on a double date; the blondes who showed up hours late, when they bothered at all; the heart-wringings of falling in love at every bus stop, in every shop, on every stairwell—all those silky-legged, smooth-faced, fluffy-haired females just beyond my fingertips, carousing my dreams like streetwalkers.

Not until I was thirty did I understand anything whatsoever about women, if I may risk such a claim. My most useful discovery was that the more mature a woman becomes, the less important to her are a man's looks and height; and the more meaningful becomes his ability to accommodate her innermost longings. Once I had sort of figured that out, I was able to dump my self-consciousness like a pair of trousers which no longer fit. But life is tricky. No sooner do you reach one inter-personal plateau when you start questioning the value of the achievement: What was so important about coupling with a secretary here, a waitress there if you didn't have anything to say to each other afterwards? Thus began my quest to enter into that human state of affairs in which two souls utterly unsuited to each other—in age, heritage, interests, temperament, education, religion—conjure up the need to construct a house of cards together . . . while having the audacity to promise each other it will stand up to the winds of change forever.

* * *

At thirty-three I found Gwendolyn. Or did she find me? as has been suggested by more than one member of my family. Fresh as a just-plucked daisy, she popped into the restaurant in response to my hand-written HELP WANTED sign. This was well after the business had been passed on to me by default, my father's heart having given way in the act of serving others. In five minutes she was hired. Jackie the cook, abandoned mother of two, hinted with a knowing sneer that the young woman was taken on so quickly because of her copper-colored hair, her turquoise eyes, not to mention her filled-out white sweater. But it so happens Gwen had been a weekend hostess/cashier at Junior's, and was also attending night classes in accounting. She was experienced, wanted to improve her skills, and was available for part-time work, so she was hired—period. It is entirely a matter of fate that, one month later, her bow-shaped lips and sing-song voice set off a strumming within me.

Without letting Jackie of the grill or Bill of the counters or Joan of the tables in on our secret, Gwen and I started dating. A movie, a ball game and, would you believe, the Museum of Natural History. Over the next half year we held hands, we kissed, we touched, we said we loved each other, and we rolled over and under each other in bed as circumstances permitted.

Though not necessarily in that order. Under shadow-stained ceilings I went so far as to tell her about my love life—not all of it, though I would've loved to gloat over every surrender that had been granted to me: It took me long enough to accumulate a past, so I hated to keep any of it to myself . . . Setsuko, Bonnie, Jeanne, the amazing Babs! But I'd kept the best stories under wraps, having learned along the way that kissing-and-telling can set off more headaches than it's worth to your ego.

As for Gwendolyn's past, it's crazy, it's illogical, it's unfair, but in those early months—when our feelings were at their most volatile—the slightest hint that she had experienced anything conclusively sexual made me turn green, downright sick. Whereas Gwendolyn seemed to care only mildly about what had transpired between me and the bodies of other females—as long as it was in the past and stayed there. When it came to current threats, however, she went crazier than me: like the time Babs Sleat swiveled her hips into my restaurant and plopped her breasts on the counter like they were the lunch special. Just as I was about to place a cup on the counter before her—Babs was a customer, after all, Gwen swept behind me and jolted my elbow, dumping steaming coffee all over the woman's lap. Very embarrassing to me, very amusing to Gwen, very painful to Babs. That was the last I ever saw of that generous, two-time divorced, two-timing dame.

* * *

Seven years ago, on May 12, Gwendolyn Loch and Alexandros Dropoulos Jr. were called upon to appear at the edge of a close-cropped, pale blue—the same color as on the Greek flag—carpet beneath a gilded dome of the Orthodox persuasion. St. Demetrius was punctuated with slats of color-stained glass, hand-polished brass implements on the altar, and a bucket of white carnations set out for the occasion. Without this enormous concession by Gwen's family—permitting these ceremonies to take place in a wholly Greek environment—there wouldn't have been any joy, any peace: My mother, aided and abetted by my aunts Harriet, Delphinia, and Merrula, would have made life ghastly for everyone. Fact is the Lochs were too pleased to marry off the last and eldest of three daughters to air their disappointments publicly. Plus they would've had a tough time negotiating which of their own religious persuasions should dominate the rites.

To marry me Gwendolyn had to suffer the indignity of answering a host of spiritually-challenging questions posed by Father Nick, and then having her forehead dabbed with a blessed rag dipped in a basin of Holy Water. It was a bogus baptism that was supposed to wash those other two religions out of her brain: If only early teachings could be washed away that easily. But it had to be done, Delphinia insisted, otherwise "the wedding wouldn't count." All this seemed to bother me more than Gwen. In fact, with a lifetime of friction in her household between a Presbyterian and a Lutheran—not as close in their thinking as I'd always imagined, she had seemed eager to become linked with a religious heritage as foreign from her own and as homogeneous as mine. However, it took less than a year of marriage for her to throw this "forced conversion" in my face.

To make sure no one at the altar got itchy feet, both families showed up in division strength, filing row by row down the pews, my family on one side of the aisle, hers on the other. Mother Evangelina stood staunchly upright in the first row, first seat, but had distressed me for months afterward by never smiling, never crying, never allowing her face to express any sentiment throughout. She could just as well have been a Baptist who had dropped in simply to see how "foreigners" conducted such proceedings. But I knew the true meaning of her deadpan silence: No matter how long she lived, she would never quite forgive me for marrying outside our faith, our culture. As it turned out, she was too much the mother figure to give up on us forever, fully expecting that down the road of life we would bear her a grandchild or two, or three. At which time she would immediately cast a net over those young minds, like fishermen in Pilos Bay. Sadly, Evangelina never accepted that the longer Greek children swam in American waters, the more difficult it would be to haul them in.

At the altar, from under a storm of white hair, underlined by still-black eyebrows, Father Nick uttered a few words in Greek and English; and Gwen, done up in a floor-length, crinoline-stiffened gown, said two words; and I, fitted into a suit that reminded me of black stove piping, said two words; and the audience whispered a few words to each other in their respective tongues; and a gaunt, pebble-gulleted deacon, aloft in a rounded balcony, chanted in Greek; and I forced a thin gold band on her next-to-last finger; and we pecked each other's puckered mouths; and that, for better or worse, was that.

After Gwen had reclaimed the bouquet of tiny pink flowers from one of her sisters, we led a procession of witnesses along the shoe-imprinted carpet, my brand new wife more or less holding up her new husband since my knees had acquired the consistency of rice pudding. Church bells were clanging. Through the double, three-inch-thick doors—heavy enough to keep the devil out, according to Father Nick, we wobbled. At the top platform the two of us were backed up against the black iron hand rail as a blur of vaguely reminiscent human beings kissed our cheeks and/or shook our hands and/or walloped my shoulder. My Aunt Harriet shocked me by planting her sticky lips square on my mouth, and one of Gwen's cousins leaned out of the procession and muttered in my ear, "Go easy on her, tonight, you hear me?" I remember thinking this dumb ass must've thought Gwen was a virgin. Later, when that dumb ass didn't appear at the reception, it occurred to me he might not have been a member of her family after all but a leftover from her private past; if so, he must've known this tempting woman was many miles beyond virginity.

At last Gwen and I were permitted to step down the wedges of granite, where all those witnesses had lined up along both sides, no longer segregated by family ties. The rice stung our faces like hail and, as we descended, I wondered if the rice-throwing was an American or European custom. Years later, even that tradition fell away—frowned upon by one group or another of concerned citizens; despite the good intentions behind the change, it now seems a significant loss, for the stinging cheeks served as a useful reminder of the pleasure and pain that lay ahead for all newly joined couples.

At the bottom step, Gwen turned her back on the cluster of women, young and old, who had gathered there expectantly, and tossed the bouquet backwards over her shoulder. It came to rest, as if directed by divine guidance, into Harriet's bony, terribly experienced hands. What could God have possibly had in mind, I wondered, by dropping the bouquet into Harriet's possession, my aunt having already had far too many husbands for one lifetime? The bells had stopped ringing the moment the bouquet landed, and I found myself scanning the crowd. It took me several moments to realize I was searching for the bulky figure of Alexandros, Sr., wondering what he would've thought of God's deliverance of those flowers into the clutches of his detested sister-in-law.

A gang of bullies—that's how these eager witnesses struck me—rushed us into a low, black, twelve-seat Lincoln, which murmured away from the curb and led a sluggish cruise of Chevys and Fords and Plymouths, not to mention my own Pontiac, along Atlantic Avenue, the Brooklyn-Queens Expressway, Metropolitan Avenue, Jamaica Avenue and, at last, Hillside Avenue . . . the way the dead are given a last tour through their former stomping grounds. In our back-wash we left an assortment of traffic snarls and red-faced, foul-mouthed motorists before pulling up at the reception hall, in the guts of

Queens, only a couple of miles from where I had done some time wearing off the tread on my Keds' sneakers as a child. A tender fascination I felt in surveying the bony trees and rounded curbs of my days of leaping without looking, a couple of decades earlier—running away from Mrs. Rhinosos, the neighborhood witch; chasing a Spaulding high-bouncer that had been blasted by Pete's swing of a sawed-off broom handle; playing Parcheesi on Toby's porch as it poured, the rain cleansing the city's streets as its accumulation rushed along the gutter like a wilderness stream.

* * *

Amazingly—blessedly the Lochs had continued to keep their mouths shut when my family designated Athena's Banquet & Catering Hall as the site of our feast, with its olive-oil impregnated menu. The Lochs gave in to my family's reception plans for the same reason they'd said very little about the selection of the church, the guest list, the printing of invitations: All three of their daughters were finally safe in the arms of matrimony, or so it pleased them to think. Moreover, since the Greeks seemed to be taking control of food distribution in America one hot dog stand, one coffee shop, one banquet hall at a time, both sides were relieved when almost-uncle Theo stepped up to the plate and offered to pay for the works. Four months later, when Theo was no longer squiring Aunt Delphinia to cheap Chinese restaurants and free concerts in Prospect Park, and the bill still hadn't been paid, Evangelina declared indignantly: "No dowry, and her people expect *us* to pay for wine and lamb!"

The catering hall was owned by Constantine Stolikes, a kind of Peloponnesian Charlie Chaplin who, it has been rumored, is remotely related to me. AB&CH was housed in a 200 by 200-foot square, windowless stack of eight-inch concrete blocks; no attempt had been made to cover up its new-world exterior ugliness with a smear of old-world stucco. The interior was another matter: Each corner was guarded by a ten-foot, plaster of Paris Doric column, painted the color (from someone's memory as weak as a twice-used tea bag) of the Aegean. The heavy-duty linoleum, by Armstrong, was a gray-stone effect laid in, according to Aunt Merrula, because it suggested to Constantine a stony path on the island of Skyros, where his great grandparents had been born. Lighting was utterly American—hospital-white, aluminum, honeycomb racks of long, tibula-like fluorescent bulbs strapped every twenty feet. The skin-pink walls were favored by eye-blue framed pictures of the ruins of the Parthenon and sword-bearing Spartans with great beards. A pair of pedestals flanked the double steel-door entrance-way, each bearing a plaster statuette—one of Apollo, god of music and poetry, the other of Aphrodite, goddess of love and beauty. Staring with embarrassing awe at this display, I could see that Greeks had been losing their sense of self as a people much the way I would be losing my sense of self in matrimony. I understood the overload of bad taste was the byproduct of an attempt to revive a long-dead state of cultural greatness, but one that had become increasingly exaggerated through the years by minds far too removed in time and space to ever approach a reasonable facsimile of that ancient grace.

My family swallowed these environmental maladjustments with abundant, unabashed pride. Dressed in a pale violet, frumpy drape, Evangelina bounced over to her sisters' end of the table to appropriate a tray of celery stalks stuffed with cloves of garlic mashed into crumbled feta, and exclaimed: "See how gorgeous is everything!"

Harriet and Delphinia shook their heads passionately: "Very ritzy!"

Semi-uncles Augie and Theo said nothing, did nothing but pop black olives into their toothy mouths and masticate on the white bulbs of scallions. It was unclear if they didn't comment on the surroundings because they had better taste or simply because they were bored.

At another table, Aunt Merrula was too busy pampering her thuggish, overgrown sons, Henry and Harry, reunited for the first time in years, to pay much attention to local embellishments.

The Lochs and their ilk, austere souls with an aptitude for severely controlled responses, were banished to wobbly tables at the deep end of the hall: They seemed to be cringing in the environment, as if someone were blowing a trumpet directly into their ears. Yet Mr. and Mrs. Loch were themselves worthy inclusions in this display of decorative monstrosities. Though tall, he was so stiff and blank-faced, with splotchy skin and wormy gray hair, he seemed short and insignificant. Though short, she was so tight-skinned and angle-boned, gaping suspiciously at it all from under a clump of mahogany-dyed roots, she seemed outlandishly tall. Complicating their physical irregularities were their spiritual improbabilities: While he was the Scot of the clan, she was the Presbyterian, and while she was the German, he was the Lutheran. Which may explain the deep sense of disorder that came over me whenever I saw them together. I found it impossible to imagine any coupling between that couple—especially with such positive results. Like Gwendolyn, her younger sisters Lucy and Penelope were as pretty as the first day of spring weather. Their husbands, Bruce and Tony, were darker, but seemed to possess a sense of humor by having shown up for the occasion. I cannot explain those lovely by-products of the Lochs' canvas necks and icy fingers any more than I can explain the attraction that binary stars are said to have for each other.

* * *

Dozens of folding tables, draped with lacy-edged paper, were bow-legged from the burden of too many platters of heavily peppered feed and pitchers of foamy or sparkling beverages. The star of the spread was the lamb, giving Jesus (the Lamb of Lambs) a fitting prominence at the feast, and this bloody flesh was dished out in a stunning number of configurations—sliced, chopped, braised, roasted, minced, broiled, mashed into paste. Rings of mint jelly were stationed at opposite ends of each table, accented by twigs of mint leaves. Last but not least were the sugar-coated almonds in a snatch of white veil, tied up with a white satin bow and set beside each person's plate. This *koufeta* is the traditional nest of good luck offered at all respectable Greek weddings, with its smooth pink and blue, egg-shaped candies standing for soft, warm, loving days and nights, and symbolizing the fruits of such loving.

Not one but two bands—one American, one Greek—hammered away at opposite ends of the hall. Their respective noises clashed midway in the huge hall, much like the cultures they represented, slamming especially hard those celebrants who were unfortunate enough to be seated in the middle. The Yanks did four or five rock 'n roll numbers, interspersed by occasional sentimental favorites—over and over; the Spartans dusted off "Never on Sunday" once every half hour, intermixed with current *bouzouki* hits which tended to numb the brain with their plink-a-plink-a-plink. But the main concern was not their repertoire, nor musicianship, so much as how good they were at playing without sleep. From what I heard after our honeymoon, the two bands didn't stop making a racket until first light had struck them silent. This must've left everyone feeling the families had hired the best bands available anywhere, at any price.

Nearly everyone got tipsy, if not flat-out drunk, as is customary at any of our profane feasts, and if not on wine, beer, anisette, and retsina, then on the thick, exhaled air that dripped over the festivities: a stirring of high feelings, sweaty armpits and crotches, cigar smoke, evaporating alcoholic beverages, and the vaporizing stench of our collective breath. . . . And of course everyone ate too much—wide flat noodles and eggplant slathered with chopped-up meats and damp blocks of feta cheese and hard-boiled eggs soaked in beet juice and mounds of vinegar-marinated olives and garlic-rubbed red peppers and slabs of pistachio-packed layers of filo. By nine or ten o'clock beef and rice wrapped in grape leaves and soggy *spanakopita* and stiffened layers of *moussaka* and shattered sugar-powdered cookies were strewn over the tables and floors like torn bodies following a battlefield massacre.

After the slaughtering of food and drink had stopped amusing them, and after Gwen and I got it started—upon their unanimous insistence, with a fox trot to "Love is a Many Splendored Thing," a favorite of hers, most everyone got up for one number or another and hoofed around the floor in the center of the hall. At times they danced so furiously it seemed as if they were acting out a pagan ritual. Toward the Witches' Hour even the Lochs arose, pressed as nearly belly-to-belly as they could manage with their angle-iron frames, doing what struck me as a kind of Scottish tango to "Somewhere Over the Rainbow," its idyllic message blared through the bell of a baritone sax and thumped on the teeth of an accordion. . . . Everyone ate too much, drank too much, danced too much, and stayed up much too late, notably the swarms of skipping, racing, yelling, brawling children—the only ones who truly had the stamina to survive such an orgy. It was almost as much fun as the funeral of Uncle Stavros.

In the wee hours Gwendolyn and I--no longer remembered as the reason for this gathering, collected our shocked bodies and shrunken brains and disconnected ourselves from that wild bunch of sacrificial lambs. This despite their demands that we shuffle "just one more *syrtos*" across the dance floor, or plant "just one last smackeroo" on each other's mouth. Pushing through the double doors made me feel as if we were breaking out of prison. The settling dampness in the cyclone-fenced-in parking lot slapped my face into startled alertness. Gwen carried the sweep of her gown over one arm like a serpent's tail as we made our way across the slick, tarred surface that had been polished to gold in places by the glare of the catering hall's blinking yellow sign.

Into the Pontiac we bent, pulling away into the depths of our first night of marriage, heading toward our three-room apartment, in Brooklyn Heights, to spend the night before driving south to Vero Beach for a week. (That honeymoon location had been chosen, I can now safely confess, because the Brooklyn Dodgers used to hold spring training in that Floridian community.) Maybe I should have paused before shifting into gear, amidst the plushness of the moment, and given my wife that one tender, prolonged kiss in private to launch us safely into our new life. But human that I am, I did not think to do this. As we rolled along a deserted Queens Boulevard, all I did was wonder if my mother had finally permitted herself to release a few of the tears she'd kept bottled up in her sockets.

* * *

My bride unlocked the door of our apartment, and when I offered to hoist her off the floor and carry her over the threshold, she laughed and led me into the darkness by my fingertips. Across a living room the shape of a railroad car we wandered, surrounded by an assortment of mismatched furniture that made the place feel like a Salvation Army thrift shop. There hadn't been time to express our own tastes, so the families got us started with a mixture of their cheerless histories: a pre-World War II set of kitchen table and chairs resurrected from the Lochs' basement; a dusty, stained tan sofa from some cousin or other; Aunt Delphinia's black-and-red Oriental wardrobe with hand-painted peacocks—which we had tried to avoid like poison ivy; a couple of butcher-block-shaped chunks of wood my mother claimed were night tables made in Greece; someone's orange rug that smelled of Pablum. Only the mattress and bed frame had been chosen and purchased by us. Home?

Gwendolyn flowed through the bedroom into the bathroom, where she had apparently arranged her wedding-night attire earlier. I halted alongside the low-slung bed, whereon we would undergo, I earnestly hoped, thousands of rounds of touches and squeezes and sighs and oaths. Along with enough tears to know the difference between happiness and sadness, as Teena Rolleck had written in my graduation album. I began to pry apart the brass studs on my starched shirt. Though the bed had been in place by the window for two weeks, we had refrained from lying in it together out of reverence for the first, officially sanctioned coming together—a symbolic attempt to become virgins for each other.

Before I had peeled off both of my socks I felt her standing behind me, and I turned to look: Pure and perfect she appeared just then. With the lamp behind her aglow, she turned her body that I might better observe her uplifted *kallipygoi* silhouetted through the pink gauze which covered her like a veil of mist. Even in my stunned state, even as her lover of more than a year, I did not fail to recognize the spectacle of loveliness she represented: the childish smile which was shockingly close to gratitude, her hair brushed over her left shoulder into a shining proof of her devotion to the moment. Nothing more and nothing less than my own Aphrodite.

Minutes did not elapse so much as drop away in clusters that night or, rather, that morning: Holding onto each other tightly, through the window panes we witnessed the tail of the Milky Way as it unwound imperceptibly over our rapidly shaping destinies. As our lips brushed across each other's ears and shoulders and necks and mouths and breasts—both of us too numb from a full day and night of histrionics to feel very much, Brooklyn Heights sent us up a wedding gift: the fragrance of dew-coated leaves, and the mellow glow on our ceiling from a corner lamppost, and a pair of soft moans from a tugboat in the harbor, and the faint transmission of rubber wheels whirring like the planets . . . the city already astir with the preparations of a new day.

From the firmness and deepness and dampness of our bodies we drew not merely sensations but a sense of the ages, as if we were in fact unfolding to each other for the very first time, two thousand years earlier, on a bed of straw in a tiny village in Macedonia. Thus we entered into an inter-locking of limbs, a blending of moistures, an interlacing of spirits: Warm fragments of stars scattered over our naked bodies, and for a time we overcame the awful separateness with which each of us had been sent into this world.

The Witch's Baptism

No doubt a few stray aunts, sundry second cousins, and over-zealous neighbors had already taken up places within finger-dipping range of St. James's massive marble baptismal basin, a sculpture so imposing it may well have been stolen, along with the Elgin Marbles, from the Parthenon; and Father Nick, his tidal wave of whitening hair in danger of crashing onto his creased forehead, must have been glancing repeatedly at the bright chrome watch on his hairy wrist: It was two-thirty and the immediate families of Dropolous and Loch—not to mention the honored, littlest guest—should have arrived half an hour ago. Worse yet, we were still a long way from being ready to leave my mother's house, and we had a long drive ahead of us, for though we had moved out of Brooklyn years earlier, we had never given up on our loyalty to St. James, better known to us as St. Demetrius. Meanwhile various members of two entirely different families were gathering in its pews for a wedding at three, and two things a guardian of holy rites does not want lumped together are a christening and a wedding. But in the confusion of rounding up some dozen-plus bodies, so we could cram our pressed suits and starched dresses into assorted vehicles and rumble off to church, we had lost my sixteen-week-old son.

"You had the baby last!" scowled Mother Evangelina, in the direction of my mother-in-law, Felicity, whose hand had already gripped the front doorknob to make her way to their bulky black Buick.

"Not me!" cried Mrs. Loch.

"I saw you leave the bedroom with the baby when I was coming up the stairs."

"I most certainly did not!"

"What about the aunts?" said Gwen's sister Lucy.

"The aunts?" Aunt Delphinia whined. "No one will let me near my nephew."

"What about Gwendolyn's sisters," offered Aunt Harriet, peering from under her leafy green hat at the two fair-haired young women. "I saw them tickling the baby under the chin," she said, her tone oddly suggestive of foul play.

Gwendolyn seemed on the verge of laughing out loud, as if she was the one who'd been tickled. Without a word she went down the hall and up the stairs, heading toward my old bedroom where the baby had been gurgling and sleeping and eating and wriggling in the bassinet—enjoying a steady supply of attention and liquid refreshment.

"Everyone just walks off," I chuckled, "and forgets to bring the only one who really matters at a baptism."

Just then my wife cried out upstairs: "My baby's gone!— he's really gone!"

I looked toward the stairs, still smiling. "A kid doesn't just evaporate," I called to her. "Not even one that small."

"That's what you think," Aunt Merrula said darkly.

Back in the living room, where there was more elbow room for accusations and recriminations, voices grew louder and more dramatic, reverberating from the buckled ceiling to the petrified wooden floor to the gravestone-shaped windows. In the meantime Gwen had dashed downstairs, into our midst, and demanded: "Who's got my baby?"

Several of the accused held out the palms of their hands to prove they weren't hiding anything. That's when it finally hit me that the baby actually had been misplaced, and that, being the father, I was the person expected by everyone to take charge. But the best I could do was declare: "Father Nick's gonna have a hemorrhage if we don't get to the church soon."

The mention of that pious firebrand seemed to ease our paralysis, and the pack of us swarmed up the stairs, down the stairs, opened doors, closed doors, ran into rooms, out of rooms. Harriet searched behind the sofa; Lucy and Penny crawled under beds; Merrula waved a flashlight beam into the attic from its doorway, not daring to cross over the threshold; grandmothers Evangelina and Felicity yanked open cabinets in the kitchen and pantry; Mr. Loch stuck his head into the baby's hamper and carriage—one in the shape of a frog, the other fleecy as a cat. Delphinia concentrated on hall closets, top and bottom; Uncle Augie, professional cynic, checked out the furnace.

And my wife and I ran around double-checking all of them.

Only my cousin Peter remained in place in the living room, refusing to look as ridiculous as the rest of us. After all, how could an infant have made its way into any of the places they were searching? Unless . . .

The irony—there always seems to be an irony handy to add richness to absurd human activity—was that Gwen and I had waited far too long to get the baby named in a holy sanctuary, putting it off for some good and some not-so-good reasons nearly four months. As each week passed my mother had assured me, in progressive order, it was a shame, a disgrace, a sin, a disaster, etc.; and Merrula, bless her gloomy hide, was going around whispering that the child would turn out evil because Original Sin "sticks to the skin" if it's not washed off with holy water within seven weeks. Why not six or eight weeks? I wondered sarcastically. But it was my fake uncle Christos who forced me to drop the superior grin: He said that if a child should be "taken away by God" before being christened, the child would be doomed to be raised by the devil "down below." (His wife Euthalia nodded in agreement vigorously.) He actually pointed at the floor, jerking his long finger downward several times as if doing a jig. Not that there was any more reason to believe his folklore than Merrula's. It's just that Christos was such a sober soul; everything he said vibrated with a sense of truth. So when we'd finally gotten around to making arrangements at the church, and inviting people, and setting up the party to follow the baptism, it was a big relief to all concerned—me as much as anyone else. Now that the baby had turned up missing, however, I was tempted to consider seriously Merrula's assessment: "God is punishing the parents for waiting too long."

A man who had both patent leather shoes lodged firmly in this world offered a more temporal explanation: "Kidnappers," said Uncle Augie. I only wish he had merely dabbled privately with this possibility –hadn't said that word aloud, reinforcing the most exotic fears of the family.

"Oh my Lord!" yelped the grandmothers, in harmony for the first time all day, as Gwen aimed a perplexed gaze at Augie, then at Merrula, then at me.

"Let's not get carried away," I cautioned everyone, at which time tears came spilling down Gwendolyn's cheeks. "My baby," she moaned, "my baby."

While I tried to make my wife understand our baby had to be somewhere within arm's reach—"It's only common sense, Honey," my own chest had come down a few notches: an increasing weight of distress that something awful had indeed happened to my tiny, helpless son. But I kept this notion to myself, wearing a valiant smile as I stood around as helpless as the rest. Unfortunately, the others were not shy about describing their fears, pushing Gwen and me and reason further and further apart.

The phone rang, silencing the bunch of us. I'm sure we were thinking the same thing: The kidnappers were calling in their demands. Encircled by both families, I whispered into the tiny holes in the mouthpiece: "Who is this?"

"Oh, it's you, Father Nick."

The families released a collective sigh.

"Yes, yes, I know, Father. I'm very sorry. There's been a slight mix up–we're trying to straighten it out right now. . . . Yes, I think you'd better go ahead with the wedding, and then we'll–oh, you've got a funeral at four. . . . Well, how's about five for the baptism?. . . . Thank you, Father, we'll try our best. . . . No, I mean we'll be there–one way or another we'll see you by five."

Inspired by Father Nick's aggravated tone–plus a new outburst of opinions around me, I stepped up on a footstool and shouted "Everyone just shut up!"

No one obeyed me, as usual, so I jumped off the stool, grabbed my grandfather's gnarled cane–left in the umbrella rack after his death like a memento of his crankiness, swung the cane high, and smashed the ancient globe fixture above with a great crash. That light hadn't worked as far back as I could remember, but had been allowed to continue collecting dust in part because Peter, the antiques dealer of the family, had once suggested that in addition to dust it was also collecting value. If the globe was worthless, as I suspected, it did serve one last, useful purpose: It restored order–without injuring anyone. But it was not the flying glass that shut them up so much as the destruction of an heirloom going to pieces, and were it not that her only grandchild was lost, I'm certain my mapou would have used that cane on me.

I almost apologized for getting their attention in that extreme way, but I felt too upset by then to be contrite. "Listen," I pleaded, "we're running around like a bunch of cats without tails. We've got to go about this systematically."

All three of my aunts glared at me fiercely: I'm not sure if they reacted this way because they had relied all their lives on their spiritual reserves to solve problems, or if they thought I was suggesting we should behave more like some other sect during a crisis.

"The last time I saw the baby was"—I checked my watch: ten to three—"maybe half an hour ago, when Gwen was laying out his christening suit in my old bedroom. Somebody had to be with the baby between the time I came downstairs and the time we realized he was—" saying the word made me compress inwardly—"missing."

"Penny," said Gwen, her makeup eroded but dry, "you went up to see the baby around that time."

Gwen's sister conceded this but said she had given way after a few minutes to Delphinia.

"All I wanted to do was bring the baby a piece of feta cheese," my aunt Delphinia declared defensively, "but your mother barged in and crumbled the cheese in my fingers."

Felicity Loch was resolute: "Cheese is loaded with bacteria."

Turning to Gwen's mother, my aunt snapped, "It's only goat's milk; that's the best thing for a baby."

Before Mrs. Loch could counterattack Gwen said, in a tremulous voice: "What happened when you were in the bedroom, Mom?"

"All I did," Mrs. Loch testified, "was gather some of the baby's things for the trip to church, but just as I was going down the hall to the bathroom I saw Evangelina rushing into the baby's room."

"I was only going to peek in on him before going to my own room to get my hat." She pointed to the black pill box on her head.

"Anyway, you were holding the baby," Evangelina accused, aiming a finger at Mrs. Loch. "Too much everybody picks up the baby."

"No! No! That bundle you saw was the bunting. The little one had dribbled all over it and I was taking it to the bathroom to wipe it clean." Mrs. Loch wiped a rusty strand of hair off her speckled forehead. "When you came up the baby was still in the bassinet."

"He's not there now," Merrula pointed out, flashing her eyeteeth.

Lucy's husband, broad-chested, easy-going Tony, tried to sum up the proceedings. "That means the baby was alone for a short time."

"The baby was alone," I repeated stupidly.

"Couldn't have been more than a minute or two," Mr. Loch said. "After I let in your aunt downstairs I went into the kitchen and drank the last of my coffee. Then I went upstairs. Gwendolyn, you were in the hall outside the baby's room. After I visited the bathroom, I walked downstairs, and you were still carrying the bunting."

"Without the baby?!" Gwen nearly shouted.

My mother-in-law screeched back at her: "The baby was gone from the bassinet, and since I'd seen Evangelina going towards the bedroom as I was going into the bathroom, I naturally assumed she'd grabbed my grandson. Everybody picks him up too much."

"I didn't touch my grandson," declared Evangelina with an alarming arch to her neck, like a cobra about to strike.

Then Augie and Christos, Harriet's current and might've been husbands, got into a squabble over whose responsibility it was to keep an eye on the kid. Of course they were really arguing about something else entirely.

"Quiet down!" I roared.

It was Penelope's soft urging, "Take it easy, Alex," that made me realize I'd become slightly hysterical, a reaction which only served to trigger another blast of hysteria from Gwen: "Who stole my baby?!"

Gwen's sister Penny, though younger than everyone else, seemed the only mature soul in the room: "Daddy, which aunt did you let in before you went upstairs?"

"Anna, I think she said."

Harriet snapped, "We got no aunt named Anna in this family."

"Yes, I'm sure she said Anna. Anna Rhinoceros, or something like that."

An ensemble of Merrula, Evangelina, Delphinia, and Harriet groaned starkly, and I verbalized what they were unable to express: "Mrs. Rhinosos is not an aunt. She's a witch." It wasn't something I actually believed. But under that ceiling of emotional chaos I wanted to believe it—at least it would have provided an explanation to what otherwise seemed inexplicable.

Grunts and fretting and chuckles (the latter contributed by Penelope's husband, tall and lanky, good-natured Bruce) filled the deep, stuffy room as Evangelina offered a brief history of potions and portents and disappointments relating to Anna Rhinosos, concluding: "No man would ever have her, so we began to call her Mrs. out of kindness." My mother summed up her story by claiming, "Mrs. Rhinosos has been trying to steal the bloom out of a child's face for many years with her Evil Eye. Alex, too, when he was a boy!"

Suddenly we were all yelping and blaming again. Mass madness it was, especially considering that Mrs. Rhinosos resided a long way off in Queens and, if still alive, was very old by that time; she hadn't been heard from in years. Perhaps it was all this insanity jammed into that narrow space that impelled me toward the telephone and, nearly knocking the instrument off its designated table, I dialed the police. The sight of me twirling a few digits stalled the bizarre dance they'd been performing, and every eye, wet or dry, turned on me.

"Hello, yes, I want to report a kidnapping—yes, I said kidnapping!" half shouting the word.

"Tell them how little he is!" Gwen screeched.

Trying to wave her off, but without success—she hovered over me—I somehow managed to provide all the information requested by the police clerk. Once I'd finished, the mad dance churned up again, only it was more out of control than before, swirling around the room and accompanied by bellows and screams and tears, lots of tears. Especially from my wife.

Unable to take it anymore, I sprang out the back door to plant my feet on grass for a few moments, hoping to establish solid footing in my perspective too. And there they were, beyond the twisted, barren apple tree: Mrs. Rhinosos and my sixteen-week-old, unbaptised son. It had never occurred to me—to any of us—that he could have been carried just a few feet outside. Our minds would only permit us to think that if he'd been taken out of the house, it had to be far, far away.

Mrs. Rhinosos had walked into the house and straight up the stairs; and in the confusion, the one or two people who happened to notice her had assumed she had a right to be among us. Into the empty bedroom she went, picked up the baby, stepped down the back stairs, out the kitchen door, and into the yard. Planned or not, her timing had been brilliant.

Sitting in a rusted outdoor rocker, the witch looked as hunched over and as coil-haired as I remembered her from my childhood, with more wrinkles than ever. Even her saucer-brimmed hat, with its crushed paper lily, seemed left over from those days. My baby, buttoned up in a frothy white suit, was giggling joyfully as the woman famous for her empty life held him close against her broad chest. Afraid to frighten her into doing something peculiar, I stepped softly over the grass up behind them, and was about to reach down and snatch the child out of her arms when she said, without looking back at me, "Your son, he is beautiful. What is the name you will give him?"

I stiffened and stuttered, "John . . . Christopher."

"Good strong name for good strong baby." She sighed, looking long into my son's face, which was pink with laughter and sunlight . . . no shadows whatsoever of Original Sin.

As I stood there wondering how she'd heard about the baptism—second-hand through one of my mother's visits to the old neighborhood, I supposed—a gang of relatives came bursting out of the back door of the house, growling audibly, teeth bared. I made a face and raised my right hand like a school crossing guard. Mr. Loch, Harriet, and Bruce stopped short on the grass. But Merrula kept coming.

"You'd better not take another step," I threatened.

My aunt froze and suddenly looked hurt—looked very human, the way she used to look before she'd begun to find evil everywhere. It was almost as if, for just a moment, she saw that evil existed more in her own mind than in the world.

I never felt a single pinpoint of coolness touch my hands or face, so I didn't realize it had begun to rain until I saw the dots of wetness spreading on the paper lily stuck into the old woman's hat.

"Mrs. Rhinosos, would you like to come to the christening?"

Faded green eyes of another place and time she turned on me, and said in a child's voice, "Ah yes, Alex, I'd like very much."

Mrs. Rhinosos began pressing her black witchy shoes into the grass, rocking the chair gently back and forth, never allowing her eyes to move away from the baby's face. Watching intently, my family, flat-footed on the hardscrabble lawn, didn't speak, didn't stir. Not until a figure in a dark blue shirt and trousers emerged from the back door, Gwendolyn right on his heels; his eyes were sharp, hers wild. Fleetingly I mistook him for a man of the cloth, but then I noticed that the heel of his hand was resting on the handle of the gun in his holster. This time I raised both arms high, and frantically waved him off. Everyone stopped, except for Gwen, who pushed past the policeman, forcing me to intercept her midway across the lawn by wrapping my arms around her shoulders. Though she kept wriggling to break loose, I managed to hold onto her long enough to allow my son to remain in Mrs. Rhinosos' arms a while longer: In the wider scheme of the universe, the baby was as much hers as ours.

Epilog

Still standing in the 21st century, I often think about what has become of my family. Cousin Peter, and his life partner, Julius, had flown across the Atlantic, landed for a two-week stay in Athens, and remained nearly three years. This had surprised me since Peter's Greekness had never seemed especially important to him–and he was, don't forget, the son of Aunt Harriet "the nomad," the least likely of us to stay put long enough to be identified as Hellenic. In a couple of handwritten letters to his mother, Peter described the old country's "bleached, rough-edged, unquenchable splendor," while also recounting the circumstances of modern-day citizens of Greece, "some of whom seem to be breaking down like the magnificent ruins of their great past."

Several in my family, including my mother Evangelina, were never struck by the desire to break away from the concrete-coated boroughs of New York City, while her sister Harriet traversed America's heartland freely as if to compensate for those who had remained rooted on the east coast. Ultimately, however, like many another who set out to conquer this continent's western frontier, she returned with this or that lost soul and set up house in New York, where our family's American adventure had begun. And of course for many other families of many other cultures.

Ya-Ya, Papou, Uncle Stavros and my mystically astute Aunt Merrula were lowered into the crusty, crowded earth of Brooklyn and Queens, while Aunt Delphinia, whose kindness had long ago established her as my favorite, took off, it was said, for Chicago, where thousands of Greeks had dug in for the long haul of becoming citizens of a culture in ascent. While Mary had died young, I haven't the faintest notion what became of my other cousins—Henry, Harry, Pavlos, and quite possibly others unknown to me. No idea whatever happened to uncles Augie or Kosmas, but our half uncle Christos is still holding hands with his wife Euthalia.

Along our marital way Gwendolyn and I added two birth certificates to New York City's Hall of Records—John Christopher and Iris Evangela, both of whom sprang out of childhood so nimbly we didn't particularly notice they were missing until their escape to state college. Today Iris teaches history on an Indian reservation outside Tucson, Arizona, and our son is an assistant to a veterinarian near Madison, Wisconsin—growing up he'd been terrified of Brooklyn's hyperactive gray squirrels. John married Grace—a dark-haired Jewish beauty from Alabama, and Iris has lived with Kiku, her Kenyan partner, for more years than we ever knew—he's a certified Honda mechanic with a Masters in French history. Together our offspring added three more Americans to the voting rolls. Gwendolyn and I didn't get to see any of them very much, which is how things are done in America today; in Greece, Evangelina used to tell me, the parents and grandparents of the Old Country, squatting under the same roof, couldn't get out from under their children's and grandchildren's feet. Back then the entire family worked long hours to mend and haul fishing nets, pluck figs into baskets, stomp on grapes, sweep the houses of the wealthy. Even so, having small replicas of themselves hanging around had seemed more of a blessing than an encumbrance in that place and time which is so far away it hardly seems to exist any more.

Maybe those early Greeks had it right. Not having our children around very long may have been, in part, why Gwen and I found it necessary to pursue separate routes in the journey of life. Not that we traveled very far—me to the Bronx, a subway ride to Yankee Stadium, where I occasionally sit in the bleachers and allow the sun to splash over my face as if it were glinting off the Mediterranean. And Gwen settled on the edge of Parsippany, New Jersey, with her second husband—a data analyst from East Berlin, Kurt Blahnecht, a decent fellow who apparently listens more attentively to Gwen than I ever did; they set up home in a split-level where, curiously, they cultivate grape vines in their backyard.

As for the rest of those who are still with us, we will be buried in American graveyards, or, as is becoming increasingly popular because it's more economical, cremated: If so, our ashes will be shaken into porcelain containers mass-manufactured in China and set on shelves where they will soon go unnoticed. Too bad we couldn't have our ashes brushed into those glorious urns shaped by the gifted artisans of ancient Greece. Certainly that would be my choice of transfer from this world to the next.

Acknowledgments

The author wishes to acknowledge, with gratitude, the publication of nine stories from *Profane Feasts* in the magazines indicated, with some of them receiving minor alterations by the author for this edition:

"The Miracle of Uncle Stavros"/*The Saturday Evening Post*

"The Devil Loves to Roll the Dice & Play a Hand of Cards," "The Occupational Rehabilitation of Cousin Henry," "The Witch's Baptism," "A Gaggle of Greek Braggarts Living with Poverty" /*Ellery Queen Magazine*

"My Father, a Philosopher in Love"/*The Iconoclast*

"Growing Up with the Evil Eye," "Ya-Ya's Declaration of Independence"/*The Smith Quarterly*

"The Truth is Risen"/*Sterling Magazine (Canada)*

An unedited, incomplete, token print run of *Profane Feasts* was brought out in Canada by Scarlet Leaf in 2017.

About the Author

TOM TOLNAY is the former editor of *Back Stage*, the film/tv/ theater weekly newspaper. More recently he founded Birch Brook Press, a small book publisher in upstate New York where he printed letterpress editions of literary titles.

Two of his novels, *Celluloid Gangs* and *The Big House*, were published by Walker & Company. Six story collections by Tolnay were published by Silk Label Books, Smith Publishers, Scarlet Leaf, and Atmosphere Press. The author's individual works have appeared in more than two dozen literary and consumer magazines, including *Saturday Evening Post, Ellery Queen, Alfred Hitchcock, Downbeat, The Fiddlehead, Chelsea Review, The Iconoclast, Confrontation, Southwest Review, North Dakota Quarterly, Carpe Articulum,* etc. His short stories have been anthologized by Dell, Signet, Down East Books, Literal Latte Books.

Tolnay's story, "The Ghost of F. Scott Fitzgerald," was first prize winner of *Literal Latte's* national short story competition. Subsequently it was produced as a short film by Sea Lions Productions, and was screened at the International Film Festival in Toronto, and at festivals in Hollywood, Savannah, and Woodstock.